Rio's hand
shoulders,

Without makeu... ...shower, her hai... ...bun and with a... ...she was the most desirable woman he had ever seen. Rio glided his hands over her upper arms, but he wanted more. His hand moved to the back of her towel, pushing her toward him. She connected with his body, by design this time; she was soft and small, her curves fitting perfectly to him, as though they'd been designed for one another.

Her lashes were too dark, feathered fans against her flushed cheeks. And the small moan she made sent his pulse into overdrive. Would she moan when they made love? Would her pillowy lips part, breathing those sweet sounds into the air?

His need was a tsunami inside him, crashing inexorably toward land. She was the shore, she was the anchor, and he was powerless to fight the pull of her tide. Rio had never considered himself powerless before. But he didn't care.

He lifted his hand to her face, cupping her cheek and sweeping the pad of his thumb over her lower lip. Her eyes flew open, pinning him with the same tsunami of need that was ravaging his defenses. "We shouldn't do this," she said quietly, but her hips pushed forward, moving from side to side in an ancient, silent invitation.

His fingers plaited through her hair, pulling it from the bun, running through the ends. "We shouldn't," he agreed darkly.

Clare Connelly was raised in small-town Australia among a family of avid readers. She spent much of her childhood up a tree, Harlequin book in hand. Clare is married to her own real-life hero and they live in a bungalow near the sea with their two children. She is frequently found staring into space—a surefire sign she is in the world of her characters. She has a penchant for French food and ice-cold champagne, and Harlequin novels continue to be her favorite ever books. Writing for Harlequin Presents is a long-held dream. Clare can be contacted via clareconnelly.com or her Facebook page.

Harlequin Presents

Bought for the Billionaire's Revenge

Visit the Author Profile page
at Harlequin.com for more titles.

Clare Connelly

INNOCENT IN THE BILLIONAIRE'S BED

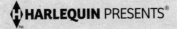 HARLEQUIN PRESENTS®

Recycling programs
for this product may
not exist in your area.

ISBN-13: 978-0-373-06124-2

Innocent in the Billionaire's Bed

First North American publication 2017

Copyright © 2017 by Clare Connelly

Printed in U.S.A.

HARLEQUIN®
www.Harlequin.com

INNOCENT IN THE
BILLIONAIRE'S BED

Amy Andrews—it was friendship at first sight.

PROLOGUE

IT WAS STRANGE that here, on an island where she'd spent only a few weeks of her life, Rio should feel so close to his mother. It was almost as if her presence roamed the walls of the shack, or drifted in off the salted waves that were rolling towards him. He didn't see her here as she'd been at the end, so weakened and ill. Here he imagined her free, running across the sand, her laugh tumbling out of her of its own volition.

He cradled his Scotch, swirling it slightly so the ice chipped against the glass. The sound was swallowed by the surrounds of the island. The beach, the birds, the rustling of the trees. Even the stars seemed to be whispering to one another—and there were so many stars visible from this island in the middle of the sea, far from civilisation.

Rosa had loved it here.

He didn't smile as he thought of his mother.

Her life had been shaped by loss and hardship, right to the end. And now he sat on the island of the man who could have alleviated so much of that pain, if only he'd bothered or cared.

No.

The island was no longer Piero's.

It was Rio's.

A too-little-too-late offering that Rio sure as hell didn't want.

Even now, a month after his father's death, Rio knew he'd been right to reject him. To reject any overtures at reconciliation.

He wanted nothing to do with the powerful Italian tycoon—never had, never would. And as soon as he'd offloaded this damned island he'd never think of the man again.

CHAPTER ONE

'CRESSIDA WYNDHAM?'

This was the time to correct the lie. To be honest. If she wanted to back out of this whole damned mess, then she should just say so here.

No, I'm Matilda Morgan. I work for Art Wyndham.

But her back was well and truly against the wall this time. What had started out as an occasional favour for the high-maintenance heiress had turned into an obligation she couldn't really escape. Especially not having accepted thirty thousand pounds for this particular 'favour'. She'd been bought and paid for, and the consequences would be dire if she didn't go through with the plan.

Besides, it was only for a week. What could go wrong in seven sunny days?

'Yes…' she heard herself murmur, before recalling that she was supposed to be acting the part of an heiress to a billion-pound fortune. Mumbling into her cleavage wasn't really going to cut it.

She lifted her head, forcing herself to meet the man's eyes with a bright smile. It froze on her face as recognition dawned.

'You're Rio Mastrangelo.'

His expression gave nothing away. That wasn't surprising, though. Illario Mastrangelo was somewhat renowned for his ruthless dynamism. He was reputed to have a heart of ice and stone—he walked away from any deal unless he could get it on his terms. Or so the stories went.

'Yes.'

The speedboat was rocking rhythmically beneath her. Was that why she felt all lurching and odd? She looked to the driver of the boat—a short man with a gappy smile and weathered skin—but he was engrossed in his newspaper. No help there.

'I had expected to meet with an estate agent,' she said, because the silence was thick and she needed to break it.

'No. No agent.' He stepped into the shallow water—uncaring, apparently, that his jeans got wet to just below his knees.

No agent. Great.

Cressida had been explicit that there would be.

'It's going to be you, some man from an estate agency, and whatever servants come with the island. Just tell them all that you want to spend time on your own to really get a sense of the place and then relax! You'll get to chill all day, get fed gourmet meals— perfect holiday. Right? It's no big deal.'

No big deal.

Only, looking at Rio Mastrangelo, Tilly thought the exact opposite was true. He was both a big deal and a big deal-*maker*, and she was hopelessly out of her depth even in the crystal-clear shallows that lapped against the side of the beautiful boat.

'Have you got a bag?'

'Oh, right...' She nodded, reaching for the Louis Vuitton duffle Cressida had insisted on Tilly bringing.

Rio took it and lifted his eyes to her, a look of glinting curiosity in his expression.

Her stomach rolled in time with the waves. He was far more handsome in person. Or maybe she'd never really paid proper attention.

She knew bits and pieces about him. He was a self-made real estate tycoon. He'd been on the news about a year earlier, interviewed because he had bought a large parcel of land in the south of London to develop. She remembered because she'd been glad; there was a beautiful old pub there—one of the oldest in London, with wonky floors and leaning walls—and she'd worked there for a summer after she'd left school. The idea of it being knocked down had saddened her, and Rio had said in the interview that he intended to rejuvenate it.

'You travel light,' he remarked.

Tilly nodded. She'd thrown a few bikinis into the bag, along with a pair of flip-flops, a few books, and some of her go-to summer dresses. Perfect for a week alone on a tropical island.

He slung the bag over his shoulder and then lifted a hand towards her. She stared at it as though he'd turned into a frog.

'I can manage,' she said stiffly, wincing inwardly at the prim intonation of her words.

Cressida was definitely not prim. A snob of the first order, yes, but prim...?

Please. Cressida's antics generally made a trip to Ibiza look like a visit to a retirement village. Cressida's father—Tilly's boss—had been thrilled that

Cressida had shown a little interest in the business finally, and agreed to visit this island and scout it as a potential hotel site.

Rio Mastrangelo wasn't Hollywood handsome, Tilly mused as she moved towards the dark stairs that dipped into the back of the boat. Not in that boy-next-door, blond, blue-eyed way that she usually found impossible to resist. Nor was he corporate and conventional, as she would have expected. He was…wild. Untamed.

The words came to her out of nowhere, but as she risked a sidelong glance at him she knew instantly that she was right.

His skin was a dark brown all over, and his lower face was covered in a thick stubble that spoke of having not shaved for days, rather than an attempt to cultivate a fashionable facial hair situation. His eyes were wide-set and a dark grey that would match the ocean at its deepest point. They were rimmed with thick charcoal lashes, long and spiked in curling clumps. His hair was jet-black and it turned outwards at the ends, where it brushed the collar of his shirt.

He had the kind of physique that spoke of an easy athleticism. He was tall, broad-shouldered and leanly muscled. His forearms flexed even as he held her bag.

It was those eyes, though, she thought, turning her attention back to the twin masterpieces in his face.

She felt as though she'd been slapped. They locked to hers: grey warring with green. The boat lurched again. She reached down to the polished timber rail to steady herself, her manicured fingers running over it for strength.

She'd chosen a simple dress for the flight to Italy.

It was a designer brand, but she'd picked it up in a charity shop a long time ago—before this crazy plan had even been hatched. It was turquoise—her favourite colour. It complemented her eyes and set off the auburn highlights in her long cherry-red hair. And her skin, though nowhere near as deep a tan as Rio's, looked golden all over. She'd chosen the dress because it looked good on her and she'd wanted to look good. But not for Rio.

She'd chosen it for the photographers who might snap her passing through Rome's airport, or travelling on the ferry to Capri. For the tourists with cell phones who would recognise Cressida Wyndham, her doppelgänger, en route to a luxurious Mediterranean holiday. She'd kept her head bent, as though she really was an heiress avoiding attention, but she'd courted it at the same time.

She'd chosen to wear the dress for those reasons.

For Rio, she suspected, she would be safer wearing a nun's habit.

Anything to discourage his eyes from drifting over her in that slow, curious way they had.

She understood the speculation in them; she'd met enough men in her twenty-four years to know what interest looked like. Cursed, in many ways, with the kind of curves most women would kill for, Tilly had long ago come to despise her generous cleavage, neat waist and rounded bottom. There was something about her figure that seemed to signal to men that she wanted to strip naked and jump into their bed.

The boat shifted again, as a wave rolled beneath it, and she paused, reaching for the rail once more. The driver had backed it as close as possible to the shore but even so it wouldn't be possible to disembark from the boat without getting her feet wet. She slipped her shoes off and hooked them with her finger, self-consciously aware that Rio was watching her from the shallows of the ocean.

She stepped down, and at the bottom moved to disembark from the luxury craft. But she mistimed it—badly. Another wave rolled and she lost her footing, stumbling almost completely into the water.

Rio caught her, of course. With Cressida's bag hoisted safely over one shoulder, and taking only a single, long step in Tilly's direction, he swept his arm around her back at just the moment she would have gone completely underwater.

He pulled her upright, his eyes crinkled with mocking amusement.

He was even more devastatingly handsome up close, where she could see the freckles that danced on his aquiline nose and appreciate the depths of his eyes, which weren't just grey. They had flecks of black and green in there too, swirling together in a combination of shapes and colours that she could stare at all day.

'I thought you could manage?' he prompted.

Tilly was stricken. What a fool she was! Cressida would *never* have fumbled such a basic manoeuvre as exiting a speedboat. No, Cressida would have taken his damned hand when he'd offered it and run her fingernails over his palm, encouraging him to stare at her all he wanted. Inviting him to do much more than that.

Matilda Morgan, though, was a Grade A klutz. Falling off a speedboat was just the kind of thing her twin brother Jack would have laughed about, and she would have joined him. Tilly never missed a chance to be amused by her own lack of finesse.

She heard the amusement escape from her mouth as a giggle at first, and then finally a full-blown laugh, though she lifted a hand to cover it.

'I'm sorry.' She smiled up at Rio, lifted a hand around his neck in an automatic response. 'I'm perhaps the clumsiest person you'll ever meet.'

Her laugh, and the admission of a lack of coordination hot on its heels, caught him unawares.

When Art Wyndham had said he'd be sending his daughter Cressida to complete an inspection of Prim'amore Rio had felt mixed emotions.

On the one hand, the beautiful heiress was known to be vapid and uninterested—he suspected he'd have her desperate to buy the island in a day or two at the most. And on the other, from what he'd heard of the mogul's daughter, Cressida Wyndham was the kind of woman he had only ever found good for one thing. She was all beauty, no substance, and she was the last person he'd willingly spend time with—except, possibly, in his bed.

But he had to admit her laugh was lovely. Like music and sunshine.

Still smiling, she pushed away from him, standing on her own two feet. 'I'm fine,' she assured him. 'Just a little wet.'

He made a guttural noise of agreement and then released her abruptly. 'You can dry off inside.'

He nodded towards the shoreline and for the first time her attention moved to the island. It was lush and green, right in front of them, but a little way further down she could see dark red cliffs that were bare of greenery. High above them there was more red, like ochre, and then in the distance the hint of trees—cypress, olive and citrus, she guessed. Back down on the coastline the sand was crisp white in both directions. Only one building broke up the expanse of beach.

A boathouse of sorts, it was of simple construction, a cross between a cabin and a hut. It was whitewashed stone, and the window frames had been painted a bright blue at one time—though a lot of the paint looked to have chipped off now. There was a small deck at the front, with two cane armchairs propped on either side of a small card table. A jaunty pot plant that had clearly been tormented by the wind stood sentinel at the door, though it had grown heavily in one direction, casting a diagonal shadow. To the side of the cabin a motorbike was propped, and beside it a speedboat on a trolley, smaller than the one she'd just stepped off—or rather leaped off into the ocean.

It was on the tip of Tilly's tongue to ask Rio what the building was, but he was already moving towards it. Sand clung to his bare feet as he strode easily across the beach. She didn't rush to catch up. Not because Cressida wouldn't rush, though she wouldn't. Tilly was captivated by the beauty of this place and she wanted to savour this, her first opportunity to drink it in.

Halfway between the shoreline and the cabin she stopped walking altogether. A light breeze trembled past her, but it was a hot day and it brought welcome relief to her through her wet clothes. She stared up at the sky, her eyes noting the colour—a glistening cerulean blue.

'It's beautiful,' she said to herself.

But Rio caught the words and turned. Her dress was saturated all the way to the top. Did she have any idea that she might as well have been standing on the beach completely naked, for all the fabric did to hide her body? Her red hair was trapped in a messy bun on top of her head but he was pretty sure it wanted to be free, to fly down her back as it might have done on Boudica or one of Titian's models.

He turned back to the cabin, his jaw clenched.

Of *course* she knew how alluring she looked. Cressida Wyndham had made flirtation an art form. He didn't really know anything about her, and nor did he read the gossip magazines, but he did know that her name couldn't be mentioned without the implication that she was an entitled, spoiled tramp with little morality.

And for some reason that angered him now.

He paused at the steps that led to the deck. They were timber, built from one of the trees that covered the island.

'What's this?' she asked, her green eyes, almond in shape, moving across the frame of the hut.

'Where we'll be staying.'

Where we'll be staying? Her heart skidded against her breastbone. Surely he'd meant *Where* you'll *be staying*? Though he spoke English fluently, his voice was accented. It wasn't inconceivable that he'd made a mistake.

Because this place was definitely not going to accommodate the two of them.

He moved ahead of her and she followed.

'It was built around fifty years ago,' he said as he shouldered the door inwards. It groaned a little. It was just wire pressed against an ornate wrought-iron pattern. There was no actual door.

The heat of the day hadn't managed to penetrate the thick walls. It was cool and dark. A hallway— quite wide, given the size of the building—went all the way to the back of the home, though at the rear, she glimpsed a sofa. There was more light there, too.

'Your bedroom.' He nodded towards a room as they swept past. She had only a brief impression of a narrow single bed and a bookshelf. He nodded to another door. 'My bedroom.'

Her heart thumped harder.

'Bathroom.'

She peered in as they walked past. It was simple, but clean. It smelled of him. She caught the masculine scent as they walked past and her stomach squeezed.

'And the kitchen.'

It was also simple, but charmingly so, with a thick timber bench, a window that overlooked the beach, a small fridge and a stove. There was a table with four chairs, and across the room a sofa and an armchair. Another larger window framed a different perspective of the beach.

'Your…your bedroom is…opposite mine?' The words were almost a whisper and she shivered.

'Surely you didn't think we'd be sharing?' he prompted, enjoying the blush that spread across her face and the way her nipples stretched visibly against the wet fabric of her skin-tight dress.

'Of course not,' Tilly snapped, before remembering that she was Cressida, and Cressida would never have taken offence at such a suggestion. She would have purred right back that he shouldn't rule anything out... 'I just didn't realise we'd be staying in the same house.'

His smile was laced with sardonic amusement. 'It's the only house on the island,' he said. 'Didn't your father tell you?'

She shook her head, but questions were floating through her mind...suspicions. Shortly after Cressida had said there'd be servants she'd said that Tilly would be left to her own devices. She'd made it sound like a glamorous beach retreat awaited.

Had she known that Rio Mastrangelo would be literally shacking up with her? Had she wisely decided to keep that titbit to herself, knowing that Matilda would have found it impossible to go along with such an elaborate deception in close quarters with a man like him?

'He must have,' Tilly said with a shrug, as though it didn't matter, but inside she was fuming.

If she hadn't desperately needed that thirty thousand pounds, how she would have loved to tell Cressida to go to hell!

Only she wouldn't have. She couldn't have. For, as much as the heiress drove her absolutely crazy, Tilly felt sorry for her. And the longer Tilly worked for Art and felt the warmth of his affection, the more she saw him disapprove of Cressida and ruminate on her lack of intelligence, skills and focus, and the more guilt Tilly felt—and more pressure too.

This was the first time Cressida had ever asked Tilly for more than an easy favour, though. And certainly the first time she'd outright lied to her! This wasn't going to a film premiere dressed to the nines, or slipping out of a top-notch restaurant early to divert the paparazzi's focus. This was a whole week in close quarters with a gorgeous stranger.

'And you forgot?' he responded with a droll inflection.

'There were a lot of instructions.' She forced herself back to the present, pushing aside the sticky question of just what Cressida had kept to herself to get Tilly on board with this deception. Were there any more surprises in store for her?

'Such as?'

'Such as don't fall out of boats.' The snappy response was watered down by a spontaneous smile. 'Mind if I get changed?'

Yes, he wanted to say. He liked watching her in this dress. Seeing the way it clung to her was flooding his body with desire—desire he wouldn't indulge with *her*, of course.

Yet he hadn't been himself since hearing of his father's death. His libido—something he liked to give free rein to, often—had taken a hit in recent times. Feeling his body stir to life was good. It was nice. He revelled in the sensation of anticipation, knowing that relief would be worth the wait.

He wouldn't give in to temptation with Cressida— that would be foolish. But once he left the island he'd call Anita or Sophie, or one of the other women always happy to join him in bed and rediscover some very pleasurable habits.

'Make yourself at home,' he said, with a shrug that was the personification of nonchalance.

She nodded, her eyes not meeting his. He was still holding her bag and he made no attempt to hand it over. She crossed the tiled floor until she was within arm's reach. At this distance she could see the flecks of black that marked his grey eyes, and she caught more of that enticingly masculine fragrance.

'I'll need some dry clothes,' she prompted, a smile tickling her full lips as she nodded towards the duffle.

He unhooked the bag from his shoulder and passed it to her. She reached for it without looking downwards and her fingers curved over his.

It was like being bitten by a snake.

She immediately released her grip on the bag and he did likewise, so that it dropped with a thump to the floor.

'Sorry,' she said breathlessly, as though it had somehow been *her* fault rather than an involuntary re-action to the spark of electric shock that had travelled through her fingertips and flooded her entire body.

'What for?' he murmured, reaching down for the bag.

Her frown was spontaneous. Neither Tilly nor Cressida were prone to inane, babbling apologies. 'I don't know.'

His laugh tickled her overstretched nerve-endings; it was a deep, throaty sound and she imagined his voice would be husky like that when he was driven by other emotions. A charge of awareness surprised her and she felt her nipples strain hard against the fabric of her bra.

His eyes dropped to them and his lips flickered in a droll smile of sardonic appreciation. 'Go and get changed, Cressida,' he said, dismissing her.

It was on the tip of her tongue to challenge him, *Or what?* when he replied, 'Before it's too late.'

Too late? A frisson of awareness pulsed through her, teasing her spine and making her shiver.

She took the bag from him and moved quickly down the hallway towards the bedroom he'd marked as hers.

Too late for what?

Her mind pushed away the most obvious reading of the statement—that there was some inevitability that they were running from. It was a silly interpretation, no doubt fuelled by her propensity to read far too many romance novels.

She kept her head ducked until she reached the door he'd indicated would lead to her own accommodation.

Her first assessment had been right.

There was a small bed, a bookshelf, and a hat rack near a high, small window that had geraniums in a window box, creeping halfway up the glass in an enthusiastic display of clustered red.

There was a mirror too, and she caught her reflection and moaned audibly. She looked… She might as well be naked. The fabric of her dress had turned a dark green and it hugged her tightly, moulding her breasts, her stomach, her bottom, and clinging in a V to her womanhood.

Her fingers shook as she went to remove it quickly, stripping it off her shoulders and pushing it from her body. The sight of her bra and G-string wasn't any better. Angrily she discarded them, until she was naked, still wet, but not caring.

Her phone was in the side pocket of her bag and

she lifted it out. The picture of her and Jack smiled at her when she activated it, and for a moment she felt her stomach swoop in relief. He would be okay. She'd made sure of it. This week was a small price to pay for his safety. What the hell had he been thinking?

She swiped her phone to life and flicked up the emails.

An error message appeared. With a frown, she realised there was no internet. No signal whatsoever, in fact.

A grim sense of being completely and utterly alone with Rio Mastrangelo sent a shiver down her spine.

How could Cressida do this to her? The more Tilly thought about it, the more convinced she was that Cressida had lied. But why? What could be so important that she'd orchestrate this deception? She obviously hadn't wanted to risk Tilly saying no—which she would have, had she known about this tiny shack and the drop-dead gorgeous billionaire only a wall away. Damn her!

Well, this would be the end of it. Once she got back to London she'd tell Cressida that their arrangement was at an end.

She ripped at the zip of the bag, pulling it roughly and lifting out another dress. But it was low at the front, and she didn't want to wear anything that might feed into the idea Rio had of her.

Cressida Wyndham, with her fake breasts, ready smile and casual attitude to life in general and sex specifically, would have been working out how to seduce the ruthless tycoon... But Tilly wanted no part of the man.

Did she?

CHAPTER TWO

'ARE YOU HUNGRY?'

He didn't look up as she entered; Tilly hadn't even realised he'd heard her.

'Not really.'

She paused inside the doorframe, studying him surreptitiously from behind hooded eyes. She caught the moment he lifted his head, saw his eyes running over her figure, his face giving nothing away. She'd have loved to pull on a baggy shirt and jeans, but she'd only packed frothy dresses and bikinis. She'd chosen the most conservative of the dresses—a dark blue linen that fell to her knees.

Wary of distracting him when he was in the middle of working, she gnawed on her lip for a moment. Then, 'My phone doesn't work here.'

That caught his attention. He flicked a brief glance at her. 'No. There's no cell tower. No infrastructure of any nature.'

She nodded, but one side of her mouth quirked downwards at the corner. 'What do you do in an emergency?'

'What kind of emergency?' he prompted curiously.

'Um…any kind. A band of marauding pirates

storming the beach, or any angry flock of seagulls pecking their way across the sand…'

His smile was unexpected—and so was its effect. Her tummy filled with frantic butterflies; her skin dotted with goosebumps.

'You don't think I could defend you against a band of pirates?'

She arched a brow. 'I think you have an inflated sense of your physical abilities.'

He arched a brow. 'A theory I'm willing to disprove at any time,' he promised darkly.

And now the butterflies went into overdrive, fluttering down to her knees and making them wobbly.

'I'm serious,' she said, the words stiffened by disapproval. 'What if there's a fire, or you break your leg or something?'

'I have a satellite phone.' He shrugged.

'But what about emails?'

'I can connect to it for internet access,' he said. 'It's slow as hell, but it gets the job done.'

'Electricity? Water?'

'Generator. Tank.'

Her mind was busy processing that. 'Whoever built this *really* wanted to be off the grid.'

'Not a lot of options on a deserted island,' he pointed out, with a pragmatism that annoyed her.

'I don't know… It seems like a post-apocalyptic bolthole.'

Or the perfect love-nest for a cheat and liar, Rio amended silently. How many women had Piero brought here over the years? Whispering sweet nothings about Prim'amore, promising a future he had no intention of providing.

'Do you need to use the phone?' he asked belatedly, drawing his attention back to her original query.

Fantasies of calling Cressida and unloading on her were clouds Tilly would never catch. Of course she could do no such thing. Besides, Cressida had said she was 'going to ground' until the wedding—that she didn't want to be seen or heard by anyone for the week, and that included turning her cell phone off.

Tilly shook her head, a distracted smile flickering across her lips. 'I thought I'd go exploring.'

He stood, and ran a hand through his hair. His shirt lifted, revealing an inch of tanned flat abdomen. She looked away as though she'd been burned.

'You know I only have a week, and Art is… Daddy is,' she corrected quickly, 'keen to hear what I think of the place.'

'Your wish is my command.' His voice was low and husky and her body reacted instantly, her nipples straining against the fabric of her dress, her eyes widening. And he saw. She just *knew* he was aware of the effect he was having.

'I'm fine.' She shook her head with an attempt at professional detachment. 'I can find my own way.'

His face wore a slow, sardonic grin. 'Just like you were fine to get off the boat?'

She huffed. 'That's not very gentlemanly of you.'

'What gave you the impression I'm a gentleman?' he queried softly, moving closer so that she found thoughts difficult to string together.

'Nothing,' she muttered. 'But I really will be fine. I'm just going to walk along the beach today. If I get lost, I'll turn back. Even *I* should be able to navigate my way around an island without coming to grief.'

'Still,' he said, wondering in the back of his mind why he was arguing with her. 'I'm here to show you around.'

She nodded, lifting her gaze to his face thoughtfully. She caught a flicker of emotion in his eyes that she didn't understand. 'Why?'

He shrugged. 'Because it's a big island and you could get lost.'

'No, I mean why *you*? You must have people who could sell an island for you.'

'Yes.' His mouth was a grim slash in his face.

'So? Aren't you too busy to act as tour guide?'

Rio thought of the paperwork cluttering his desk in Rome and shook his head. Contracts for the high-rise in Manhattan. The lease for the Canadian mall. The purchase offer he'd made on a mine in Australia.

It could wait. Keeping the invasive tabloid press away from his private life was priority number one. He'd spent the last five years making sure his parentage wasn't revealed, and he wasn't going to let the truth come out now. Involving more people than necessary in this deal was a sure-fire way to invite public attention.

'Yes.'

Why had he decided that distraction was the best way to get her off the scent and stop her questions? He couldn't have said, but he moved closer, noting with interest the way her pupils darkened.

'But I don't really like the idea of you drowning in my ocean. Or tumbling off a cliff on my land.'

'*Your* ocean? *Your* land? Someone's got a bit of a God complex, haven't they?'

His laugh was deep; it resonated right through her.

'Until your father signs on the dotted line, that is the truth of the matter.'

She tilted her head to one side, lost in thought. 'I don't know if I believe *anyone* truly owns an island like this.'

'I have a piece of paper that would beg to differ.'

She waved her hand through the air distractedly. 'Yes, yes—*legally*. But don't you think...?' She left the sentence unfinished as she realised what she'd been about to say. Discussing her personal philosophies wasn't part of the job. And, essentially, she was on Prim'amore to work.

She'd been paid—and paid a small fortune. Now she had to uphold her end of the bargain.

'Yes?' he prompted, but Tilly had zipped away from their conversation.

'Well,' she said, injecting her voice with the same sense of entitlement she'd personally been on the receiving end of any time Cressida had called and asked for a favour, 'if you really want to waste your time playing sales agent, then let's go.'

He arched a brow, but if he was surprised by her pronouncement he didn't otherwise show it.

Tilly did a pretty good Cressida huff as she strode down the corridor and pushed the door to the cottage open. But the moment she stepped on to the small deck she froze, a gasp escaping her mouth.

He followed, almost bumping into her. 'Problem?'

She shook her head, her eyes wide as they took in the sheer beauty of the spot. He watched her, and understood the wonderment in her face. Hadn't he felt a similar sense of incredulity when he'd first arrived?

'It is heaven on earth, mi amore.'

His mother had been confused at the end. She'd slipped in and out of her past just as a dolphin rippled over the surface of the ocean, and most of her memories had revolved around *him*. Piero. The bastard who'd broken her heart and left her pregnant and destitute.

'It is as if God left a small piece of heaven just for us to find and enjoy.'

His expression was grim as he studied the horizon, seeing it as Cressida was. The ocean was immaculate. A deep turquoise colour disturbed only by the gentle cresting of waves. The sky was a blanket of deep blue, the sun an orb of white, high in the sky.

'I feel like we're the only ones on earth,' she said with a shake of her head. 'I hadn't expected the island to be so...'

He waited, curious as to how she would choose to describe it.

'It's not just beautiful,' she said, searching for words. 'It's...magical.'

'Magical?' he repeated derisively, ignoring how close the description was to his mother's first impression.

The amusement in his tone was enough to drag her back to the present. 'Yes.' She forced a cynical smile to her face. 'At least that's what Daddy will be hoping hordes of tourists think.'

He nodded, dismissing the sense that she was hiding something from him. 'The island's perfect for a holiday resort. Close enough to Capri to provide entertainment, but totally isolated at the same time. It's easy to imagine how special any resort would be here.'

She nodded, but there was sadness in her heart. Having been on the island less than an hour, she already knew she hated the idea of buildings and roads cutting across it. Of people bobbing in the ocean, boats churning across its smooth surface, voices shouting through the serenity.

'Yes,' she said, her frown carrying into the simple word.

'What would you like to see, Cressida?' he asked, and the use of the socialite's name reminded Tilly forcefully of just what her duties were.

'I was just going to walk along the beach,' she murmured, nodding in one direction.

'Fine. We'll walk.'

He moved towards the stairs and she followed, though his presence was knotting her tummy again.

'You really don't have to come with me,' she said softly, pressing her teeth into her lower lip as she tried to calm the butterflies that were having a party inside her.

'I really *do* have to come with you,' he corrected quietly. 'For as long as you are on Prim'amore you are my responsibility.'

A frisson of anticipation danced along her spine. She moved quickly down the stairs, her feet sinking into the sand once she reached the level shore.

'Prim'amore... First love.' She glanced at him. 'It's a romantic name. Any idea of the history of it?'

'No,' he lied.

Secrets, secrets. So many secrets. Hell. *He'd* been a secret most of his life. Only in recent years had his father lifted the ban on his identity being known, and by then the exposure had outlived any usefulness or appeal.

'Why are you selling it?'

She was at least a foot shorter than he was. He adjusted his stride to match hers, shoving his hands in his pockets as they moved towards the water.

'I do not want it.'

She frowned. 'You don't want a pristine, untouched island off the coast of Italy?'

'No.'

Her laugh was carried by the breeze. He turned to chase it, wishing it was louder.

'Why ever not?'

He met her eyes, his smile feeling heavy somehow. 'I already have an island. A bigger one.' He thought of Arketà, with its state-of-the-art home and pier, the helicopter pad and three swimming pools. 'Two seems excessive.'

'And here I was thinking you to be a man who thrived on the excessive,' she heard herself tease.

At the edge of the water she paused, kicking her shoes off and bending to retrieve them. She moved closer to the ocean, flexing her toes as she reached the water's line, then stepping beyond it so that the waves caressed her ankles.

'So why buy it if only to sell? Or was it an investment?'

He looked at her for a moment, wondering at the instinct throbbing through him to speak honestly to her. To admit that he hadn't bought the island so much as inherited it. That in the month he'd possessed Prim'amore it had sat heavily on his shoulders like a weight he didn't wish to bear. That the gift was unwelcome and that selling it was his primary desire.

'Not exactly.' His smile gave little away. 'I do not need it. Your father has been shopping for a resort site in the Mediterranean for years. The match is too good to ignore.'

She nodded, but he could practically see the cogs turning. 'You said your island is called Arketà?'

'Yes.'

'I like the sound of that.'

He nodded. 'It means pretty in Greek.'

She arched a brow, her grin contagious.

'I inherited the name when I purchased it. The previous owner christened it so for his daughter.'

'I see.' Tilly nodded, but her smile didn't drop.

'That and I'm a hopeless romantic,' he responded with an attempt at sarcasm.

Tilly shook her head. 'Nope. I would bet my life that "romantic" is not a word ever associated with you.'

'Oh? And how *would* you describe me?' He prompted, curiosity leading him down a conversational path that his brain was urging him to reconsider.

She slowed for a moment, her eyes skimming across his face as her full lips pouted. She was a study in concentration and it almost made him laugh.

'I think it's better that I don't say,' she said finally, turning her gaze back to the beach. 'Do you spend much time there?'

It took him a few seconds to realise she was back on the subject of Arketà. He shook his head. 'I thought I would when I bought it.'

'But?' she prompted.

His shrug lifted his broad shoulders. She tried not

to notice the strength in those shoulders, but she was only human.

'Work.'

'Ah. Yes.' She knew the demands of Art Wyndham's schedule intimately, and could only imagine how much more hectic Rio's was. 'So you're in Rome most of the time?'

'*Si.*'

Tilly could imagine that. He had an effortless chicness about him that was completely ingrained. It wasn't an affectation. He didn't have to try. He was both masculine, wild, untamed and...handsome. Nothing about him screamed ostentation, yet he exuded power and wealth.

'And you?' he surprised her by asking.

Tilly almost lost her footing, but she righted herself before he felt the need to intervene. 'What about me?'

Out of nowhere she thought of Cressida. Cressida who was so visibly similar to her that Tilly had thought she was looking into a mirror the first time they'd met. Their red hair was long, their eyes green, their skin a similar colour—though Tilly's tanned more easily. They were both of medium height, and though Tilly was naturally more curvaceous, Cressida had bought breast and rear enhancements two years earlier, making their figures almost matching.

'I gather you've made an art form out of living fast and loose?'

Tilly frowned. As always, a whip of sorrow for the billion-dollar heiress flayed her. True, Cressida's lifestyle was a masterpiece in modern-day debauchery, but Tilly somehow just understood her. And there was a lot more to the glamorous fashionista than partying. If only she'd let anyone see it.

'Not really,' she heard herself say. 'The papers don't always give me a fair shake.'

Now it was Rio's turn to slow. He angled his face to study her profile. 'Papers make up stories, but photos never lie.'

Her heart thumped hard against her chest. Had he seen photos of *her*? Could he tell the difference? For, as much as she and Cressida were uncannily similar, they were not the same person, and it was easy to see the differences when you set your mind to looking.

Though Tilly had an answer ready for that. She wasn't wearing more than the bare minimum of make-up, and Cressida was never papped without a full face. Even her morning coffee run was completed in full glamour style. It was completely plausible to explain away the slight differences in their appearance by claiming a lack of cosmetic help. At least to a man, surely?

'I think people look at photos of celebrities and see what they're looking for,' she said softly. 'I could leave a nightclub at three in the morning, stone-cold sober, arm in arm with a guy I've been friends with for years, and the next thing you know I'm drunk and three months pregnant with his baby.'

She rolled her eyes, her outrage at such misreporting genuine. She'd personally placed enough calls to Art's solicitor, lodging complaints and libel suits, to know how frequently Cressida was photographed and lambasted for something that was perfectly innocent.

'Am I to feel sorry for you now?'

She lifted her face to his, her expression showing mutiny. 'I don't want sympathy.'

'I can see that.'

She stepped over a jellyfish, marooned elegantly against the sand, its transparent body no longer capable of bobbing in the depths of the ocean.

'So you are *not* a wild, irresponsible party girl, then?' he asked, his voice rich with disbelief.

Tilly shook her head, thinking of Cressida. She was everything Rio accused her of, and yet Tilly couldn't stomach the idea of him looking at her and seeing Cressida.

'I'm not *just* a party girl,' she said after a beat had passed. 'Honestly, I'm more comfortable somewhere like this. Somewhere away from the cameras and press. Somewhere I can just be by myself and read.'

Read? Hardly Cressida's favourite pastime, but no matter. He wasn't ever going to discover that fact for himself, was he?

'It is hard for you to be alone when you're in London?'

'Yes,' she said. But impersonating Cressida was wearing thin. 'When did you buy this island?'

His eyes bobbed out to sea, chasing something invisible and transient on the horizon.

'I recently acquired it,' he said silkily, tweaking his response slightly to fit the facts.

'And now you're selling it?'

He nodded. 'We've covered this.'

Her lips pulled downwards. 'It just doesn't make sense.'

'On the contrary—it makes perfect sense. I own an island I do not need or want. Your father desperately wants an island of this size, within easy boat distance of the mainland, and he is prepared to pay the price I have stipulated. Provided you do not go back and report that the volcano is about to explode, I will no longer own Prim'amore in a matter of weeks.'

There was more to it. Tilly could almost feel the words he wasn't saying; they were throbbing beneath her fingertips. But she needed patience to massage them to the surface.

'Volcano?' She moved the conversation to less critical ground. 'You're not serious?'

'Absolutely. It is extinct now—a relic. The lava no longer flows in its belly.'

She shuddered. 'How can you be sure?'

His laugh was warm honey on her sensitised muscles. 'Because a team of geologists have told me so.' He stopped walking and angled his whole body to face her. 'Would you like to see it?'

Her breath hitched in her throat. Staring down the chasm of a volcano would be the most dangerous thing she'd ever done. Well, almost. The more time she spent with Rio the more she was coming to realise she'd taken a step into the terrifying unknown by agreeing to pose as Cressida.

'Yes,' she heard herself agree. 'I would.'

'We'll go tomorrow.'

He nodded with the kind of confidence that had surely been born out of his success in the boardroom. Or given rise to it. She blinked up at him and wondered if anyone ever told him no.

'Not often.'

She frowned, her confusion apparent.

'I am not often told no.'

'Oh!' Evidently her mouth had run away with her—and without her permission too. She felt heat warm her cheeks and began to move again, along the shoreline, kicking the water as she went, enjoying the feeling as it splashed against her shins.

'I expect it has always been the same for you?'

Tilly thought of her family. Her parents who had worked hard all their lives, who adored her and would have found a way to give her the moon if she'd asked it of them.

'Why do you say that?' She returned his question with a question.

'Because I have known women like you before,' he said simply, shrugging his broad shoulders.

'And what's *that* supposed to mean?'

His smile was derisive, and yet her heart flipped as though he was offering her a bunch of flowers. She turned away, frustrated at the schoolgirl crush she seemed to be developing.

'That you grew up with more money than most people see in a lifetime. And that in my experience women like you tend to be...'

'Yes?' she prompted, her hackles rising despite the fact he was making assumptions about her doppelgänger, not her true self.

What had he wanted to say? Did it matter that the spoiled rich girls he'd bedded in the past were all boring, entitled, selfish and dull? Why were they talking about this?

His frown deepened. He was supposed to be showing her the island; that was all. It was the kind of thing he'd never have deigned to do under normal circumstances. God knew he had more important things to focus on. Still, he couldn't—*wouldn't*—let the press get wind of his ties to Prim'amore. Rio, and Rio alone, would handle all the contracts associated with the sale.

But it should have taken days. Not a week. Art had been strangely insistent, though. Cressida wanted a week 'to really get a feel for the place', and Art had expressed his relief that his wayward daughter was showing such good business sense.

But he didn't need to spend the whole time taking beach strolls with the admittedly beautiful heiress. And certainly not sharing his innermost thoughts.

'Never mind,' he said, his voice a dark contradiction of the light banter they'd been sharing. 'This beach stretches for another two miles before the cove curves inwards and we'll need to climb the cliff. I suggest we leave that for another day.'

He was being deliberately unpleasant.

No, not unpleasant.

Just a big, gorgeous roadblock to any conversation she tried to make.

He'd been like it as they'd walked on the beach. As though he'd flicked a switch and she no longer held any interest for him. He'd pointed out details of the island, suggested positions that might be suitable for a hotel, but he had made it clear that he felt obliged to provide her with business information and that was the end of it.

So why did it bother her?

She'd come to the island expecting to meet with a dull estate agent. She'd brought books and bathing costumes, anticipating a delicious week on her own, soaking in the sunshine and relaxing.

But now her nerves were stretched on tenterhooks.

She flicked the page of her book, even though she had no concept of what she'd read, and briefly lifted her eyes to where he sat. There was only one living space in the house and he'd taken up position on the small table. It held his laptop, and thick files spread in each direction. His head was bent, he had a pen in his hand, and as he read one of the files he occasionally scratched a note angrily in the margin.

Unexpectedly he flashed his eyes in her direction and she looked away, stumbling her focus back to reading. His eyes continued to burn her skin, though.

He stood abruptly, scraping his chair noisily against the tiles. She kept her head bent as he moved into the kitchen and she heard the fridge open and shut.

She turned the page—again with no concept of where she was in the story.

The sound of butter simmering in a frying pan finally captured her interest, and she risked a glance towards him.

Her heart stuttered. Rio Mastrangelo was a seriously gorgeous man at any time. But with his shirtsleeves pushed up to the elbows, his head bent as he chopped tomato and fennel…he was the poster boy for sexiest man alive.

'What are you doing?' she asked, wishing she hadn't when his eyes lanced her and she felt her stomach swoop.

'Stringing a fishing line,' he replied, with a sarcasm that he softened by smiling.

He had a dimple in one cheek. Deep enough to dip her finger into. She looked back at her book.

'I presume you eat normal food?' he asked, with a challenge she didn't understand in his question.

'It depends what you call "normal."' She gave up on the book, folding down the corner at the top of a page and placing it on the sofa.

She stood and padded towards the kitchen, curious as he added basil leaves to the chopping board. He reached for the fridge once more and returned with fish, adding each fillet one by one to the sizzling frying pan. He sliced a lemon down the middle and squeezed it over the top, then ground salt.

'That smells delicious,' she said seriously. 'You like to cook?'

He shrugged. 'I like to eat, so…'

Her smile was involuntary, and her attention was momentarily distracted by the sizzling fish, so she didn't realise that his eyes had dropped to her mouth and were staring at it with an intensity that would have boiled her blood.

'I would have thought you'd have a chef. No—a *team* of chefs. All ready to obey your every whim.' She lifted her brows as she turned her attention back to his face.

'No.'

More of the stonewalling she'd faced that afternoon.

'No? Why not?'

'Because, Principessa, not everyone grew up in the hyper-indulged, rarefied way you did. I learned to cook almost as soon as I could walk. Just because I can *afford* to employ chefs it doesn't mean it's necessary.'

The hostility of his statement hurt far more than it should have. He was judging her—no, he was judging *Cressida*, she reminded herself forcibly—and she didn't like it. Not one bit.

Her throat ached. With mortification, Tilly realised his harsh rebuke had brought her to the brink of tears. She took a steadying breath and looked away.

He expelled an angry breath and reached for the fish, flicking it deftly. 'I'm sorry,' he said after a moment. 'That was rude of me.'

If his judgemental bitterness had surprised her, the apology had even more so.

She lifted her eyes to him slowly. 'You think I'm spoiled.'

His smile was brief. A flicker across his face that she thought she must have imagined. He reached for two plates and scooped the tomato and fennel mixture into the middle, then added several fish fillets and half a lemon. It had the kind of presentation a five-year-old would have been proud of, but it smelled incredible. Her stomach groaned in agreement with that thought and she cleared her throat in an attempt to cover it.

'I believe you drink champagne?'

Tilly frowned, and was on the brink of pointing out that she really didn't drink much at all before remembering that Cressida was practically fuelled by the stuff. She found it perfectly acceptable to start her day with a glass of bubbles. And, despite the fact she could knock off a bottle on her own in no time, she never seemed affected by it. Which showed she had an incredible tolerance for the stuff. Unlike Tilly.

Yet she nodded, knowing it would lead to questions if she disavowed something so intrinsic about the heiress.

He reached into the fridge and pulled out a bottle—Bollinger, she saw as he unfurled the top.

'The cabin is not exactly well appointed,' he explained, pulling out a single tumbler and half filling it with champagne. He handed her the glass, then scooped up their plates and cutlery.

'You're not joining me?'

'No.'

He moved down the corridor, pushing the door to the balcony open with his shoulder and holding it for her to move past. It surprised her; she'd assumed they'd sit inside at the table.

But when she looked up she let out a sound of astonishment.

Somewhere between their walk on the beach and the pages she hadn't read, the sky had caught fire. Red, orange, pink and purple exploded in every direction, backlit by warmth and turning the ocean a vibrant hue of purple.

'Wow!'

He set the plates on the small table, his eyes following hers.

'Remember when we swam as the sun dipped down and the sky was orange? And you told me I was a mermaid who'd come from the sea?'

His mother's voice had been crackly and faint. The last of her cancer treatments had left her disorientated and confused.

'Prim'amore—my love, my first love. For ever.'

When death had been at her doorstep, she'd thought

only of *him*. Piero. A man who hadn't even come to the funeral—who hadn't so much as acknowledged her passing.

Rio compressed his lips, his appetite diminished.

Not so Tilly's.

She sat opposite him and attacked her fish with impressive gusto, pausing occasionally to turn back to the view, before remembering that she was starving, apparently, and pushing another piece of her dinner into her mouth.

A beautiful mouth. Full and naturally pouting, with a perfect cupid's bow that out of nowhere he imagined tracing with his tongue.

His body stirred at the idea. The sooner he got off this island the better. Any number of women would make more suitable, less complicated lovers than Cressida Wyndham.

'You didn't answer my question.'

He leaned back in his chair, his eyes roaming her face. 'Yes.' His nod was concise. 'I think you're spoiled.' His eyes dropped to her lips once more— lips that were parted now with indignation. 'But it is not your fault.'

'Oh, geez. *Thanks*.' She reached for her champagne and sipped it, pulling a face when the water she wanted to taste turned out to be bubbly and astringent. Still, it slid down her throat, soothing her parched mouth and calming her nerves.

His laugh sent her pulse skittering.

'I mean only that anyone raised as you were would be spoiled. You have been indulged from the first day of your life. Adored. Cherished. All your dreams made a reality, I imagine.'

Tilly couldn't have said where the need to defend Cressida came from, but it was like a sledgehammer in her side. Sisterhood? Girl power? Her own childhood had been idyllic. *She*, Tilly, was the one who had been spoiled. Not with material possessions—money had always been tight in the Morgan household—but with time and love.

'Yes, well, that may be true, but there's more to life than physical possessions, and far better ways to show affection than by giving gifts.'

Curious, he leaned forward. 'Poor little rich girl?' he prompted, and when she kept her face averted, her chin set at a defiant angle, he felt a surge of adrenalin kick in his gut. 'Have I hurt your feelings, Principessa?'

She reached for her champagne once more and held it in one hand, her eyes roaming the ocean before lifting to his face. 'You haven't hurt my feelings.'

She spoke with a calm control he hadn't expected.

'You've made me curious about yours. You haven't even known me a day and yet you speak of me with derision and contempt. That can't possibly be based on who I am, seeing as you barely know me. It must be because of who *you* are. And *your* hang ups. You think less of me because I come from money.'

She had surprised him and he hadn't liked it. *At all*.

Her insight had been rapier-sharp. He'd judged her because of what he'd presumed her to be, and that was hardly fair. He'd have never made his mark in business if he'd carried such assumptions alongside him.

He swirled his Scotch, his eyes resting on the now dark sky.

Was she asleep? She'd finished her dinner abruptly after her incisive comment and scuttled inside. He'd listened to the sound of the sink being filled and dishes being washed, all the while pondering the mystery of Cressida Wyndham.

When Art had said his daughter was coming to inspect the island Rio had instantly formed preconceptions. He knew enough about Cressida to know what to expect. But since she'd arrived she'd defied each of the ideas he'd held. She'd fallen into the water...and *laughed*. She'd accepted the humble accommodation without complaint. She'd read her book, and she'd thanked him for cooking. Hell, she'd done the dishes.

None of that fitted into the way he'd envisaged someone like Cressida behaving.

She'd been right. He didn't like her. He didn't like women *like* her.

How could someone like Rio, who'd been raised in abject poverty, feel anything but resentment for the kind of indulged lifestyle that had been made available to the Cressidas of the world?

His thoughts wandered distractedly to Marina. The heiress he'd thought himself in love with many years ago. She'd been beautiful, too, and she'd seemed interesting and genuine. But she'd taught him an important lesson: never trust a beautiful woman who cared only for herself.

He leaned back on the deck, his eyes lingering on the silver streak of the moon reflected in the water. His mother had tried to provide for him. Had she not become ill, undoubtedly their lives would have been comfortable. His expression was grim as he remembered that sensation of hunger and worry. Even as a young boy he had been sent to school in uniforms that were a little too small, shorts that didn't quite fit, shoes that were second-hand and badly scuffed.

All the while his wealthy father had refused to intervene. And now he'd given him this! A parting shot. A last insult. An island that intrinsically reminded him of Piero and all the ways he'd failed Rio and Rosa.

CHAPTER THREE

SHE WAS IN AGONY.

Being tortured alive with every bump.

The bike was old, yet powerful, and the man drove it with expert ease. Still, there wasn't a road so much as a track, and she had to keep her arms wrapped tight around his waist, her legs squeezed against his. She could feel his heart racing beneath her hands, smell his intoxicating masculinity, and her stomach was in knots.

Every hitch in the road brought her womanhood closer to him, bouncing her on the seat. Needs long ago suppressed were being pushed to the front of her mind. Heat flamed through her and it had nothing to do with the morning sun that was beating down on her back.

Tilly had never been into cars or bikes. She liked nice, smart, kind men. Men who had blond hair and white teeth and clear blue eyes. Who called her mum 'ma'am' and liked to watch the football with her dad and Jack.

Nice guys.

There was nothing 'nice' about Rio Mastrangelo, but her body was sparking with a desire she'd never felt before.

She angled her head, focussing on the view of the island as the bike climbed higher, around the track, but it was no use. Her eyes saw the glistening ocean, and the spectacular greenery between them and it, but in her mind she was imagining making love to Rio on top of this very bike. Straddling him and taking him against the leather seat.

She was ashamed of herself!

Then again, she'd woken up in a state of confusion and arousal because she'd dreamed about him. Dreams that had made her body sensitive. And that sensitivity was not being helped now, by the bumping of the bike along the road. Nor by the feeling of his powerful legs moving inside hers. The broadness of his chest and the rise and fall of his back.

She was in trouble.

Cressida might have no trouble getting into bed with strangers, but Tilly didn't do the whole casual sex thing. She wasn't a prude, but she'd never really wanted any guy enough to ignore common sense. She wanted the fairy tale. She wanted to meet a man who swept her off her feet and offered love and happily-ever-after.

Rio would never be that.

What he would be was a sensational lover.

She groaned under her breath at the very idea. Her hands, curved around his chest, wanted to drop lower. To find the hem of his shirt and push it up so that her fingertips could connect with bare flesh.

This was a nightmare.

No way could she act on these feelings! Apart from anything, she'd feel as if she was letting herself down. Where could this go? She was lying to him—

pretending to be someone she wasn't. A secret she absolutely had to keep!

It wasn't just the money Cressida had paid, though that was a huge part of it. Cressida had *begged* her to play along, and not for the first time in Tilly's life she'd felt sorry for the glamorous heiress.

'I have a wedding to go to. Mum and Dad would never approve. It's really important, Tilly, or I wouldn't have asked.'

Matilda suspected that Art and Gloria would indeed have disapproved, but that wouldn't have stopped Cressida from going. It just would have led to yet another loud shouting match, resulting in Cressida storming out and Art fretting for days over how he could handle his wayward daughter more effectively.

Having worked for Art for four years, Tilly had seen enough of those confrontations to know they were best avoided. Art wasn't in great health, and every time he lost his temper with Cressida, Tilly worried.

No, she'd saved everyone a whole heap of trouble by coming to Prim'amore in Cressida's place. After all, it was only a week. Cressida would attend the wedding, Tilly would stay on the island, and then they'd get back to their normal lives with no one ever knowing they'd performed a switcheroo.

She ignored the niggle of disquiet over that—and the inevitable conclusion that after this week she would never see Rio Mastrangelo again.

He turned the bike around a corner, leaning into it, and she leaned with him, holding on tight as the bike seemed to dip close to the grass on one side. He straightened, but she kept on holding him tight. Finally he brought the bike to a stop, pressing one powerful leg down to kick the stand.

'This is where the path stops.' His words were accented.

Belatedly, Tilly realised she was still gripping his waist and that there was no reason to do so. She jerked her arms away and fumbled her way off the back of the bike, scratching her calf in the process.

He had no such difficulty. He lifted himself off as though he'd been riding bikes all his life.

'You're a natural at that,' she said, the words thick.

He lifted his helmet off and placed it on the seat, the turned to unclip hers. 'It's not rocket science.'

'Still…' She held her breath as his fingers brushed against the soft flesh under her chin.

He reached for the clasp and pressed it; the helmet loosened and she reached up to dislodge it at the same time he did. Their fingers tangled but he didn't pull away, and nor did she. His eyes held hers for a beat longer than normal, and her stomach swooped up and then down.

She cleared her throat, pulling her hands away and smiling awkwardly. *Yeah, great.* Just what Cressida would have done, she thought with an inward groan of mortification.

He didn't seem to realise. He pressed the helmet onto the seat and then reached back towards her.

His hand in her hair was like the start of her dream coming true. She watched, mesmerised, as he studied the red lengths, pulling his fingers through it, a slight frown on his face. Her breath hitched in her throat and anxiety began to perforate that strange mood.

Had he recognised who she was? Or rather who she *wasn't*?

'Do you dye this?'

She pulled a face, not comprehending why he'd ask such a question. 'No!'

'I didn't think so.' His frown deepened. 'It's like copper and gold.'

'Yes.' She nodded, stepping backwards and almost tripping on a rock that jutted out of the ground. His hand on her elbow steadied her, then dropped away again. 'I hated it, growing up. I used to get teased mercilessly.'

'I find that hard to believe.'

Strangely, it was something that Cressida and Tilly had in common. They'd discussed the dislike they'd felt as children, for having such unique colouring.

'Yes, well—says you, who's probably always looked like a mini-Greek god.'

The words were out before she could stop them.

'I'm Italian,' he pointed out, his grin doing strange things to her blood pressure. 'And there is nothing miniature about me.'

'You know what I mean.' Her cheeks flushed bright red. She might as well have blurted out that she couldn't stop thinking about how gorgeous he was.

He nodded, apparently taking pity on her because he didn't pursue it. 'I wouldn't have teased you for your hair. Or anything.'

Her heart thumped. 'Is this the volcano?' She nodded at the jagged mountaintop that was still a little way above them.

He grinned, his eyes lifting to the peak. 'Yeah. The track stops here.'

'So we'll walk?'

'Sure.' He lifted the seat of the bike and pulled out a black rucksack, hooking it over his shoulder. 'Let's go.'

She'd packed flip-flops and dresses, neither of which were especially suited to scaling a Mediterranean volcano. But she wasn't going to complain.

'The volcano would make an excellent tourist attraction. I know the previous owner of the island had plans drawn up to run a cable car across the top.'

'That's a great idea,' she murmured.

The climb was steep and her breath was burning, despite the fact she was generally in good shape.

'Just say if you require a break,' he murmured.

Not bloody likely, she thought to herself, sending him a sidelong glance. 'I'll be—'

'Fine,' he responded. 'The thing is, you usually say that before you fall over, so perhaps we should pause.'

'That happened *once*,' she said with a laugh, reaching across and pushing at his arm playfully.

He grinned back, but it was no longer playful. The atmosphere was electric.

She swallowed, forcing the conversation to something less incendiary. Something safe. 'Was the previous owner looking at developing the island for tourists?'

Rio's step slowed. *'Si.'*

'I wonder why he didn't,' she murmured.

'He died. Unexpectedly.'

'Oh! What a shame. That's awful.'

He stopped walking and turned to face her. 'Look, Cressida.'

He nodded behind her and she spun.

An enormous smile broke across her face. 'I'm on top of the world!' she said, shaking her head.

The ocean spread like a big blue picnic blanket in every direction, but from this height she could make out ships in the distance, and another island dotted with bright homes.

'Capri,' he explained. 'It is only twenty minutes away by boat.'

'So close. And I thought we were all alone in the middle of the sea...'

She smiled up at him, but the look of speculation in his eyes stole her breath. There was no way this awareness was one-sided. He felt it too. Didn't he?

She jerked her eyes back to the view, her mind spinning, her blood rushing.

'I was wrong last night. And you were right to point that out.'

His admission had come out of nowhere. She looked up at him, then turned away again. It was like staring at the sun.

'So what is it with you and money? You have a fortune, right? Why do you have a chip on your shoulder about people like...like me,' she finished, a small pause punctuating her question as she forced herself to remember just who she was supposed to be.

'I told you. I have known a lot of women like you.'

He shook his head, clearing the image of Marina once more. The two women were nothing alike, apart from their beauty and the fortunes they'd grown up knowing to be at their fingertips.

'And yet they were not like you. They were women of the same background. I expected you to be the same. And yet you are...'

'Yes?' A breathy question, a plea for him to continue.

'Unique.' He grinned, breaking the mood that was swirling around them.

'Thanks.'

She turned her back on the view. They were close to the top now.

'You didn't have money, growing up?'

His expression darkened and she understood that he was wrestling with whether or not to answer the question.

'No,' he said after a moment, taking a step towards the precipice of the volcano.

She fell into step just behind him. 'Your parents?' she prompted, curious about this man.

There'd be information on the internet, if she looked him up, but that wasn't possible for the next week. Her phone had no reception on the island.

'My father wasn't in the picture,' he said, and the words were clipped, as though they were being dragged from him. 'My mother worked hard to make ends meet. But she got sick and wasn't always able to hold down jobs.'

'I'm sorry,' Tilly murmured, her heart squeezing. 'Is she…okay now?'

'She died. A long time ago.'

'Oh, Rio.'

She reached out and curled her fingers around his forearm, forcing him to stop. He was much taller than she was, but a step ahead of her the difference was even more pronounced.

She stared up at him, saw the sun golden behind his head. 'How old were you?'

A muscle jerked in his jaw. Her eyes dropped to it, and she understood his anguish and pain.

'Seventeen.'

She shook her head slowly from side to side. 'What happened?'

Again, it seemed he wasn't going to answer. She watched him weigh up his words and finally he turned around, resuming his course up the hill and breaking their contact.

'Cancer,' he said under his breath, just loud enough for her to catch it.

She nodded, but her heart was breaking for the young man he must have been. On the cusp of adulthood, alone in the world.

'What did you do?'

His laugh was a brittle sound. 'What did I *do*, *cara*?'

The term of endearment came without warning but she didn't question it. She infinitely preferred it to his use of Cressida's name.

'I finished school and then I worked.'

She nodded. 'And your father wasn't able to...?'

'He wasn't in the picture,' he repeated.

He stopped walking abruptly, and before she could bump into him and tumble backwards he turned and hooked an arm around her waist. The gesture was intimate; it set little flames burning beneath her flesh.

'Look.'

He nodded straight ahead and, curious, she moved in that direction.

'Don't fall in,' he said softly, from right behind her. The drop from the top of the volcano was several hundred feet, and there was a lot of stone along the way.

She threw him a withering look over her shoulder—and then missed her footing altogether, stumbling on the rocky path and pitching forward dangerously.

With an oath, he reached for her and pulled her backwards, holding her against his chest. Her breathing was forced, her heart pounding—though from adrenalin or the proximity to Rio, Tilly couldn't have said.

'You are *unbelievably* clumsy,' he snapped, but his eyes were on her lips, and his hands, firm against her back at first, were soft now, moving slightly, caressing her through the flimsy fabric of her dress.

His body was firm and hard; he smelled like sunshine and sweat. A pulse between her legs was firing wildly and her dream was playing out right before her eyes. She wanted him to kiss her. No, she wanted to kiss *him*.

Cressida would have. She would have wrapped her arms around his neck and pulled his head down, leaving him in little doubt of just what she wanted.

But, though they looked like twins, Tilly was nothing like Cressida.

'I lost my footing,' she said, not breaking their contact. 'I wasn't going to tumble to my death.'

'Mio Dio,' he said darkly, his eyes caressing her face where she wanted his fingers, his mouth to touch. 'That is exactly what you would have done if you'd been a foot closer.'

'But I wasn't,' she murmured, not sure what they were arguing about any more. 'Rio...?'

Her eyes moved to his lips and she darted her

tongue out, moistening the outline of her mouth, staring at his, needing him to kiss her.

His chest was moving rapidly, but he wasn't out of shape. It was something else that was causing his breath to explode from him.

'I feel as though I need to shadow you from now on,' he said with a shake of his head, his eyes glued to her face. 'To keep you out of danger.'

Her smile lacked humour. 'I think there's danger here, too.'

His eyes flickered with recognition. She was right. He was about two mad moments away from plundering her mouth, from tearing at her dress and laying her on the ground. Her, Cressida Wyndham, a woman he barely knew, a woman who was on the island as his guest.

He dropped his arms and stepped backwards, moving his attention back to the volcano. 'Can you be trusted to look without falling?'

He'd flicked a switch and was back to normal. As though his hands *hadn't* just been stroking her back, his legs straddling hers, his face an inch away and aching to kiss her.

Tilly found it harder to return her mind to its scheduled programming. She jerked her head in agreement, but as she stepped closer to the edge of the mountain he stayed close. Close enough to grab her.

The temptation to fake another fall was strong, but she resisted it.

'I have never seen anything like this,' she said honestly.

She hadn't been sure what to expect, but not this.

It looked as though the earth had been dug out, hollowed, and right at the bottom of the valley there was a lagoon so blue she ached to swim in it.

'I had no idea. Is this what happens to volcanoes when they die?'

'I believe each one is different,' he said.

'Can you go down there?'

He laughed. 'No. Not *you*. I think that would be a disaster.'

She sent him a look of muted impatience. 'I'm really not that bad. You must have a rope or something?'

Realising she was serious, he sobered. '*Dio, cara*, you're going to give me a heart attack. Are you seriously suggesting scaling this volcano?'

'Look at that water,' she said plaintively. 'It's divine.'

He eyed her thoughtfully for a moment. 'It does look nice. But there is nicer.'

'Yeah? Where?'

'Come. I'll show you.' He unhooked his rucksack and pulled out a water bottle. 'Thirsty?'

She shook her head. She might have been before, but other needs had subsumed everything else.

'Hungry?'

She shook her head again, but her tummy did a little squeeze.

'Well, I am.'

His smile was rueful. Beautiful. She was lost.

He reached into the rucksack and pulled out an apple.

She arched a brow. 'Really?'

He nodded. 'What's wrong with fruit?'

'Forbidden fruit,' she muttered under her breath, but his grin showed that he'd heard.

'Want a bite?'

He held it out to her and she eyed it warily before shaking her head, more firmly this time.

'Suit yourself.' He shrugged, making short work of the apple before tossing the core into the undergrowth. 'Let's go.'

Another twenty minutes on the bike did little to calm her overstretched nerves, and by the time he pulled it to a stop in the middle of what seemed to be a forest of thick cypress trees, she was almost ready to burst.

He removed his helmet and stood, but before he could reach for hers she unclipped it hurriedly, adding it to his on the seat in front of her.

His smile was droll and she had the distinct impression he was laughing at her.

'Well?' she asked, with an impatience born of embarrassment. 'What are you showing me?'

'You wanted to see some spectacular water,' he reminded her, his expression carefully blank of emotion.

She climbed off the bike, wishing she'd thought to pack some shorts and jeans. There was no neat way to dismount, and she stood pushing her dress down, only to look up and find his eyes arrested on her legs.

Heat flared inside her.

'Which way?' she asked, the question a husk in the middle of the forest.

He jerked his head slightly to the left but then his eyes met hers and Tilly felt it.

Inevitability.

She was fighting it, and so was he, but they might as well try to stave off night's fall.

This thing between them—whatever it was—was going to happen.

CHAPTER FOUR

'WELL?' HE PROMPTED, looking not at the water but at the beautiful British heiress.

Her eyes, so green they matched the ocean, sparkled. Her lashes fanned her cheeks as she blinked rapidly, looking from the trees that nestled right up to the edge of the white cliff face to the water that was a pristine turquoise.

'Oh, yes…' She nodded, crouching down and peeking over the edge. She looked away from the cliff, following the water to the point where the island separated and admitted the ocean. 'This is perfect.'

Her voice was soft and full of emotion.

Curious, he crouched beside her. 'You are upset?'

'No!' She smiled, but her eyes were sparkling with unshed tears. 'I'm…overwhelmed. Overcome. This is impossibly beautiful.'

His life had been a tribute to the pursuit of beauty; rather to preserving it. He had never met another person who felt that as strongly as he.

'That probably seems really stupid,' she mumbled, turning back to the water.

'Not to me.' His smile was reassuring. 'Well?'

She stood, sucking in a deep breath. It tasted

like Italy. Salty, sweet, with the hint of cypress and fresh air.

'Well what?' she queried, placing her hands on her hips.

'Care to join me for a swim?'

She eyed the water thoughtfully. It was damned tempting. The heat of the day, not to mention the fire raging between them, had left her with a distinctly raised temperature. A dip in the crystal-clear water would feel wonderful.

'What's the matter?' he asked teasingly. 'Don't you want me to see your underwear?'

She gasped, her eyes enormous in her face. 'I'll have you know I'm wearing a bikini,' she responded archly, but her pulse was firing again, her cheeks pink.

'So?'

He grinned, and before she knew what he was doing his fingers had reached for the bottom of his shirt and lifted it over his head. She had a second to take in perfect abdominals ridged into a broad, tanned chest, a line of dark hair that ran down the middle, disappearing into his waistband.

He tossed the shirt to the ground, then began to unzip his jeans.

She fluttered her eyes closed as desire ran rampant through her.

'You confuse me,' he said thoughtfully, a moment later.

She blinked, flicking her eyes to his nether regions and expelling a sigh of relief to see that he wasn't completely in the buff. A pair of dark boxers covered his masculinity. But there was plenty of him on display. Legs that were strong and muscular, tanned and hair-roughened.

Legs that she was imagining curling around her waist.

Oh, heck. She was in serious trouble.

'Do I?'

'*Si*. Why would you be shy about swimming?'

'I'm not shy,' she promised—but, oh, she was. Shy and exhilarated.

'I didn't think so. You were, after all, photographed skinny-dipping with about three hundred festival-goers in Germany earlier this year.'

She stared at him, not sure what to say to that. She was tempted to point out that the photographers had only *guessed* that Cressida had been naked—she hadn't been. Or to query his knowledge of gossip pieces. But that story hadn't been restricted just to the scandal rags. It had gone into the mainstream news. Even the broadsheet papers had covered it because of the timing—Art Wyndham had been meeting the President of the United States of America that same day.

'There are no photographers here. Just you and me. And I promise we will keep some clothes on.'

She sent him a withering look, but her pulse was racing. Slowly she reached up, her fingers unsteady as she hooked them into the straps of her dress and slid them down her arms. He followed their progress with his eyes and she could have sworn he was holding his breath.

The bikini she'd chosen was no less and no more revealing than her others, but when she stood before him wearing only the flimsy scraps of white fabric she desperately wished she'd put up with the heat and stayed clothed.

'Wow...' he muttered, his eyes taking their time as they trailed over her body.

'Is something the matter?' she snapped, resisting the impulse to cross her arms over her chest.

'No.' He grinned, flashed his eyes to her and then returned to his inspection of her body. 'I am just... overwhelmed.'

She opened her mouth to say something, but when he made a copycat sniffling sound she laughed and ran towards him, pushing at his chest. 'I'll make you pay for that.'

'Yes?' He grabbed her wrists and held them by her sides, so that only her harsh breath sounds punctuated the stillness. 'How do you suggest you'll do that?'

She bit down on her lip, her mind completely bereft of responses.

When he reached down and lifted her up, cradling her against his chest, she made a small sound low in her throat.

It all happened so fast.

One minute she was processing just how good it felt to be close to him, and the next he'd leaped off the edge of the white cliff. They were flying through the air.

His laugh was the last thing she heard before they hit the water.

Splash!

There was noise, then complete immersion in the water, and finally his letting her go, so that she could splutter her way to the surface.

Her red hair was straggling over her face, and she spun around, trying to pinpoint him.

'You…you…' she spluttered when he lifted out of the water, a grin crossing from ear to ear over his handsome face. 'How dare you?'

He tilted his head to one side, his eyes darkened by an emotion she couldn't comprehend. 'We have a problem, *cara*.'

'Yeah?' She could think of about a hundred! 'What's that?'

His smile lifted as he pulled one hand out of the water, something white clutched in his fingers. It took several seconds before she realised it was her bikini top.

With a squawk, she lowered herself in the water, treading water as he made his way to her.

'Give that to me,' she demanded indignantly.

'I intend to.'

He was right in front of her and she turned her back on him, embarrassment and coyness making her want to shield herself from him.

'Here.' It was a gravelled husk. A word that invited her to turn around and stare at him.

She fumbled with the bikini in the water—no easy task when she had to simultaneously kick her legs to stay afloat.

'Would you like help?'

If she'd been in a generous mood, she might have appreciated that without help she was unlikely to succeed. But Tilly's mood was all over the place.

'No. I'm fine.'

His laugh teased her, and she felt her own lips lifting in response.

'Don't laugh at me,' she responded, attempting to sound angry when actually she was being flooded by a confusing degree of happiness.

'Don't make me laugh, then,' he said simply. 'Here.'

He swam to her back and reached for the clasp of her bikini. He had every opportunity to milk their close contact, but he didn't. His fingers moved with professional detachment, clipping both the halter neck and the back without lingering.

And how she'd wanted them to linger!

'I truly didn't realise jumping into the water would lead to you getting almost naked,' he said, but something about his face made her wonder if that was a lie.

'Yes, well… No harm done.'

Such a prim expression! She winced, and for the hundredth time since arriving couldn't help but imagine how Cressida would have reacted in such a situation.

'This cove is incredible.' She changed the subject desperately, gliding through the water.

'It is quite unusual, isn't it?' He caught up with her easily. 'There are caves through there. I have only swum in a couple of them, but I understand the network is elaborate.'

'Really?' She moved towards the entrance he'd indicated, curiosity thumping inside her. 'I'd love to see them.'

'Not today,' he said quietly.

'Oh?' She turned in the water. 'Why not?'

'I have to go through some contracts this afternoon. My secretary is waiting to hear from me.'

She blinked at him, remembering that he was a

property mogul first and foremost, not really a tour guide at her beck and call.

Disappointment was a hole in her gut.

'You can go back. I'm sure I'll find my way.'

He shook his head. 'It's five miles. Swim now and I will bring you back another time.'

Another time. This was the second day of her week. It was still early. But the idea of losing an afternoon because he had to work sucked the happiness out of her mood.

'Fine.' She shrugged, duck-diving under the water and kicking away from him.

She went towards the ocean, surfacing when her lungs were burning and begging for more air to be drawn into them. He was where she'd left him, treading water.

'What are the contracts for?' she called across the water, spreading her arms wide and kicking at the ocean to stay afloat.

He moved through the water easily, his stroke that of someone who swam often. He pulled up a little distance from her. Water droplets ran over his smooth shoulders.

'A high-rise I'm buying in Manhattan.'

She tilted her head to the side, her smile spontaneous. 'Seriously?'

He flicked some water at her, smiling as she flinched away. 'Why not?'

'You already have two islands. A high-rise in Manhattan seems excessive.'

He arched a brow, and beneath the water waved his hands perilously close to her sides. She felt the tremble of water but didn't move away. Deep down, she knew she wanted him to touch her.

It was illicit. Forbidden.

Inevitable.

Hadn't she already realised that?

'I have another high-rise in Manhattan, too. And one in Hong Kong. Dubai. A mall in Canada. Is that excessive enough?'

She rolled her eyes. 'Now you're just trying to impress me.'

'I would think those assets far too pedestrian for someone like you to be deemed impressive.'

She sucked in a breath and flicked a gaze at the water. It was rippled by their movement. If only he knew that her parents lived in a small, pebbledash semi-detached bungalow in Harlesden.

'What I find impressive is that you did all this yourself,' she said with truth. 'You say your mother struggled? And she passed away when you were still a teenager? Yet by the time you were twenty you were a force to be reckoned with.'

Emotions flicked across his face, none of which she could interpret. 'You have been researching me?' he asked quietly at last, when her nerves felt as if they were about to snap.

She leaned closer, her expression conspiratorial, her nose wrinkled. 'Nope. Not even a bit. I hate to be the one to break it to you, but…'

'But?' he murmured, his eyes resting on the tip of her nose before lifting to hers.

'You're kind of famous.'

His laugh resonated around the cove. 'Is that so?'

'Well…well-known.' She grinned, her head bobbing in agreement.

Art had mentioned Rio several times. She'd listened. She'd learned. Though she had never imagined herself coming face to face with the man.

'What's the building?'

He frowned.

'In New York?' she supplied.

'It's a turn-of-the-century masterpiece,' he said with a grin. 'Art Deco, with original fittings on almost all the floors. It's on the edge of Harlem, and for a long time it was ignored, but now the area has begun to gentrify.'

'And you want to be in on that?'

His eyes were dark in his face. 'I want to stop it being knocked down to make way for yet another steel monolith.'

She nodded thoughtfully. 'You have a habit of doing that. Of buying old buildings.'

Again, she thought of the pub in London he'd saved.

'It's good business,' he said with a shrug. 'To see value in what other people disdain. It's served me well.'

She tilted her head to one side. 'I think it's more than that.'

His laugh was a rumble. Desire skittered along her spine. 'Do you? Why?'

Because she looked at him and saw something she didn't understand. Because she'd known him a day and felt as if she'd seen into his soul. Because he was a confusing mix of machismo and compassion. Because she just did.

'You bought a pub in London.'

His eyes honed in on her, waiting for her to continue.

'It's really beautiful. Old. Dilapidated. And you saved it. I think you buy these old buildings because you want to save them.'

'That's a by-product of what I do,' he agreed.

'Why don't you admit it?'

He laughed. 'There is nothing to admit.' He flicked his fingers along the water's surface. 'The first building I bought was something no one wanted. It was very cheap. I couldn't save it.'

'What did you do with it?'

He grinned. 'I thought you knew everything about me?'

'What did you *do* with it?' she repeated, too curious to exchange teasing jokes with him.

He sobered, leaning back in the water a little and staring at the canopy of trees overhead. 'I arranged to demolish it but I salvaged everything. My first business was a brokerage of historic building parts. Tiles, bricks, marble, mirrors, light fittings—even carpets.'

'How did you know that would even work? That people would be interested in buying the parts alone? I would have ended up with only a run-down old building to my name.'

'There is value in beauty,' he said finally. 'Always.'

She bit down on her lower lip, focussing her attention on the cliff face. His words had set her pulse racing, but it wasn't just him and his words. It was the island. The whispering trees. The warmth of the sun and the saltiness of the water.

'What's there now?'

'A steel monolith,' he responded with wry humour.

'Ah.' She flicked her eyes to his face to find him staring at her. Her heart skipped.

'The building in Harlem isn't just a collection of bricks. It marks a time in the city's history when man was mastering the skills of constructing homes in the sky. It is a snapshot of time, a testament to what *was*. To the strength and resilience and the wonderment of what could be. It speaks of history and hope. If we demolish all of these old buildings there will be nothing left to show what used to be.'

Her pulse fired. His words sparked passion in her blood; their cadence was a call to arms she was quick to hear.

'I agree.' She smiled at him, her enthusiasm radiating from every pore. 'London is an ever-changing city. So many of the buildings in my area have been knocked down to make way for new developments and every time I go past them I feel sad at what we're losing. Homes that survived wars don't have value any more.'

He lifted his fingers from the water. She watched, mesmerised. They were beautiful fingers. Lovely hands. Strong. Confident. Tanned. She blinked and looked away, before she did something stupid like reach out and wrap her fingers around his.

'Where did the previous owner of the island want to build the hotel?' she asked, bringing the conversation neatly back to business, desperately looking to stifle the desire that was wrapping around her.

'Not far from the cabin.' His words were spiced with an unknown emotion. 'It is an ideal spot.'

'I think you'd be hard-pressed to find anywhere here that *isn't* ideal.'

He shrugged. 'Perhaps.'

He rubbed his fingers over his shoulder, scratching at something she couldn't see.

She swallowed and looked away.

But the trees whispered above her.

Inevitable.

Don't fight it.

It's going to happen.

She sent them an angry look and swam closer to the rocks.

What did trees know, anyway?

He was right behind her, but at the same time he kept his distance. A distance that allowed her to breathe.

'I'd be interested to pick your brain on that. You've spent more time on the island than I have. Even in a week, I'm sure I won't have really got to grips with the place.'

'There are plans you can look at—plans the previous owner commissioned many years ago for a potential hotel,' he suggested, without realising what he was saying.

He caught at the offer a moment too late; there was no way to pull the words back. Rio was not a man who made mistakes. *Ever.* Yet offering up his mother's drawings was like giving her the key to his longest held secrets.

'That would be great.' She was nodding, her mind skipping several steps ahead. 'I want to put together as much information as possible for Ar— Daddy.'

That was a little bonus she'd decided on for Cressida. Thirty thousand pounds had bought Cressida a week off the radar, celebrating a wedding with her friends. But Tilly was going to throw in the kind of report that would make Art think Cressida had turned over a new leaf.

'Fine.'

Was he angry? Tilly studied him from beneath her lashes. His dark face was tilted away from her, his cheekbones slashed with colour. She wanted to reach over and trace his jawline, dip her finger into the cleft of his chin and the dimple in his cheek. She wanted to feel his stubble tickle her cheek as she ran her face close to his.

She wanted so much.

'Ready to go back?' His words were thick.

She turned to him and nodded. 'I'm ready.'

And, come what may, she really, really was.

She dreamed of Jack that night. Jack, pale and shaking. Jack, crying, his eyes dark and his cheeks stained by tears. Jack, afraid. Jack, in danger.

She saw him vividly—not through a veil of sleep and memory, but as he'd really been. As he'd been only six weeks earlier, when he'd turned up on her doorstep and told her everything.

'I made a bad bet, Tilly. A really bad bet. I didn't realise it at the time but...but the guy...the bookie...'

She'd waited, impatient and also annoyed that he'd had the nerve to rock up on her doorstep at three in the morning when she had a big meeting to attend at work the following day.

'His name's Anton Meravic. I didn't know he was hooked up, Tilly. I swear.'

'"Hooked up"?' she'd asked, not exactly sure what that meant. It had been late, after all. Her mind had been fogged by sleep.

'To the mob! The Russian mob. He's in with Walter Karkov and I owe him twenty-five thousand pounds! They're going to kill me.'

She dreamed of Jack, pale and shaking.

She dreamed of Jack, her twin.

Her brother.

Her other half.

And she woke with a start.

Her heart was racing, blood was pounding through her body, and her mind, her brain, were slamming with fear and adrenalin. The crashing of the waves echoed through her as bit by bit she remembered where she was.

Jack was safe. She'd done what she needed to pay off his debts. Thanks to Cressida, and the payment for this week's 'job', she'd been able to fix it for him.

Nothing mattered more than keeping Jack safe. *Nothing.*

Not even the strange feeling that Rio was beginning to wrap his hands around her heart and squeeze it tight.

CHAPTER FIVE

IN THE MORNING she woke early, and was still tired.

Her eyes were scratchy, her mind exhausted.

Jack.

Her sigh perforated the silence, slitting her stomach with worry and doubt.

Some people were easy to worry about. They had problems that could be understood and therefore reliably navigated. With Jack it was like a dark cloud of uncertainty all the time. Wrong turns abounded. Since they were children he'd been that way. Not a naughty child, and certainly not unkind. Just worrisome and vulnerable. He'd made poor decisions, bad friends, worse choices.

And now, at twenty-four, he was still making those bad choices.

Only the stakes were much, much higher.

She shook her head, tilting her head towards the window and staring out at the sea. The day was breaking, the sun's yolk spreading across the sky in a fog of orange and peach.

He'd be okay. She'd make sure of it.

Having paid off his debts to whoever the hell this

mobster was, she wanted to believe Jack was out of trouble for good. But that wasn't guaranteed.

She stood slowly, planting her feet against the tiled floor, her eyes not leaving the view.

What time was it?

She crept closer and then pushed the window open slowly, carefully, not wanting to wake Rio. A hint of the night's cool brushed her cheeks, kissing them pink. She breathed in deeply, catching the tang of salt and smiling despite her nightmares.

It was early and the house was silent.

She lifted her shoes off the floor and padded barefoot from her bedroom, then tiptoed down the hallway. The front door to the cabin was unlocked. She pushed it outwards and her smile widened as she emerged onto the deck. The steps were covered in sand; it felt ice-cold beneath her bare feet. She paused to slip her shoes on and then thought better of it, tossing them to the ground and walking away from the house.

The wind was decidedly brisk. She wrapped her arms around her waist as she walked, her eyes focussed on the dawning day.

The island was stunning. It almost beggared belief to find such a piece of untouched paradise in this day and age.

It wouldn't be untouched for long, though. Her lips shifted, a small frown dragging down her mouth at one side. Would the island still resonate with magic and mystery when buildings crowded it? When a cable ran across the volcano, allowing tourists to spy into the cavernous top and see its secrets?

Her frown deepened. And how could Rio care so

little about what happened to this place? Why had he bought it? And why was he selling it so quickly? He was a businessman, and he'd made a career out of preserving beautiful buildings that were in jeopardy. Surely he felt the same about nature.

Was it possible that he really didn't care what happened to Prim'amore?

She stopped walking and stared out to sea as the breeze pushed past her, lifting her dark red hair and whipping it into the air behind her. She wanted answers. Not because it would change a damned thing. Art would still buy the island and do what he wanted; and Rio would sell. She didn't think she had a chance to change their minds. But that didn't mean she couldn't ask questions. Curiosity was alive inside her, begging for release.

Her hair was a flame. It shifted with the wind, creating contrast with her pale skin. He stared out at her, transfixed. The morning sun was bathing her with its buttery light and she looked soft and sweet.

Sweet.

Hardly a word he'd thought would ever apply to Cressida Wyndham.

He watched as she swooped down and lifted some sand into her fingers, then spread them wide to let it sprinkle on the ground like billions of pieces of confetti. Even at this distance he could see her smile and the way it shone across her face.

Her eyes shifted, moving towards the cottage, and despite the fact he was looking through a window, he moved away. The impulse to hide made him laugh.

Rio Mastrangelo didn't run from anyone.

With a guttural sound of impatience he stalked out of his bedroom and into the kitchen, pressing a pod into the coffee machine and watching the thick, dark liquid pool into a mug. He paused it mid-flow, needing just a hit of caffeine and the taste of something other than desire to warm his gut.

So she was beautiful. Stunning. Sexy. That he had expected. But, knowing what he did about her lifestyle, he'd thought her charms would hold little appeal.

That belief had been scuppered by a hard-on he'd been grappling with since they'd swum together yesterday. Since she'd turned her back and waited for him to clip her bikini in place. Her skin had been so smooth beneath his hands. How he'd wanted to reach around and cup her breasts, to stroke her nipples and ease her backwards against him so that he could trace kisses along her neck.

It had been too long since he'd been laid. That was all. For a man used to indulging his virile libido whenever he wanted—a man who had any number of women lining up to join him in his bed—a month of abstinence had been a spectacular feat. Being in close proximity to a woman like Cressida, with her body men would go to war for, was like pouring gasoline into a room and leaving a packet of matches by the door.

He just had to move the matches.

'Oh! You're up.'

She smiled as she breezed into the kitchen, smelling like sand and sunshine, and looking like a water nymph who'd risen from the depths of the sea, her

long hair tangling down her back as he'd imagined it
the first time they'd met.

He reached for his coffee and sipped it without
dropping his eyes from her face. 'It's almost nine,'
he pointed out.

'Right.' Her cheeks were pink, as though she'd
been running. 'I've been exploring.'

It was such a conspiratorial confession that he almost laughed. The urge to chastise her for going on
her own, without him to save her from plummeting
off cliff faces, died in the face of her obvious joy.

'Have you? And what have you found?'

'Just the most beautiful island,' she said, with a
smile that was lit from inside.

The gasoline dripped closer to the matches.

'I can't believe how lovely it is here.' She eyed his
coffee thoughtfully and then walked, barefoot, into
the kitchen. She left little drifts of sand in her wake.
'Mind if I make a coffee?'

He shook his head. 'Of course not.'

'Would you like another one?'

Surprise at the simple courtesy flared. 'No. Thank
you.'

The machine made its tell-tale groaning noise as
she brought it to life and waited for coffee to fill the
cup she'd selected.

'Do you have those plans? I'd love to take a look
at what the architect came up with.'

His expression gave little away. 'They are somewhere here.'

Mischief danced in her eyes. 'Is that like a clue?
Am I to hunt them out, *à la The Secret Seven* or *The
Famous Five*?'

He stared at her blankly and she rolled her eyes.

'Please tell me you've read them?'

'Read what?' He was lost.

'The books! Enid Blyton mysteries.'

He shook his head, dragging a hand through his hair. 'No.'

'How deprived your childhood must have been!' She laughed, and then sobered as she recalled his claim that he'd had nothing growing up. 'I didn't mean… I meant… Oh, crap.'

She clamped a hand over her mouth and speared him with a look of such bewilderment that he burst out laughing.

'You think you have hurt my feelings? That I am crying inside?'

She dropped her hand and looked away, back to the coffee. How ridiculous she was being! Talking to him as though they were old friends, teasing him about not having read Enid Blyton books and reacting as though she, Tilly Morgan, had the power to hurt him! Rio Mastrangelo! The man who was renowned for his ruthless cold temperament.

With effort, she shoved her enthusiasm and delight deep inside her and assumed her best mask of casual arrogance—just as she'd seen Cressida do a thousand times.

'I'm serious about those plans.' She cradled the warm mug in her hands.

He stared at her for long enough that the air began to crackle around them. Time stood still, but her emotions did not. They were a fever in her blood. Uncertainty, lust, confusion, danger.

She bit down on her lip, and then stopped when his

gaze lowered, his eyes knitting together as he traced the outline of her pout with heavy eyes.

Uh-oh.

Her heart was pounding hard and fast.

'I am going to Capri later today. Would you like to come and see it?'

The question came to her from a long way away. Her mind was jelly. She swallowed, but her pulse was throbbing so loudly that she wasn't even sure she'd heard him properly.

'Capri?' she murmured, shaking her head slightly from side to side.

Rio stood and prowled towards her. There was no other word for it. He was like a powerful animal stalking its prey, his eyes hooded as he gained ground, closing in on her. He hooked his mug beneath the coffee machine, his body only inches from hers. So close she could feel his warmth. A shiver danced along her spine.

'I'm sure it's not like your usual haunts. Only a few nightclubs. No couture boutiques that I know of…'

Her cheeks flushed and her eyes met his beseechingly. He was determined to think the worst of Cressida. It shouldn't have bothered her. So why did she find herself wanting to plead the other woman's case to him?

'No, thanks.'

His eyes narrowed speculatively, as though he'd been expecting her to jump at the chance to get off the island. She gathered it hadn't entered his head that she might prefer to stay where she was.

'I'd prefer you to come.' The words were a gravelly command.

She arched a brow, her eyes jolting away from his. 'As much as I'm here to fall in with your every wish, I want to stay on the island. And look at the plans.' Her tone was unwittingly belligerent, but it was a pretty good impersonation of Cressida's.

He reached for his coffee, his forearm brushing against her in the process. She started, flames of need dancing through her.

Her nerves stretched, pulling tighter. 'Have fun, though.'

He scowled. 'You don't think you should appraise the island for yourself?'

'That's what I'm doing,' she pointed out, her heart hammering. Pride kept her where she was, but her sanity was urging her to step away. Far away.

'Capri, I mean,' he corrected. 'Its proximity to Prim'amore is a point of interest. I imagine your father would want to hear your thoughts on it and the crossing.'

Her eyes were wide in her face. Damn it. He had a point.

'Come on,' he murmured, as a snake charmer might. The words were enticing, seductive, impossible to ignore. 'It will be a quick trip, and afterwards I will find the plans.'

She ground her teeth together. 'Are you blackmailing me?'

He grinned. The butterflies were back—a whole kaleidoscope of them.

'Yes.'

'Why do you want me to come with you?' She asked, dropping her eyes to the ground between them.

The silence was a thick, knotted ball. When he spoke, the words seemed almost dragged from him.

'That is a good question. And I'm not sure I have an answer to it.'

Her heart turned over. Agony and pleasure warred in her heart. 'Okay.' She nodded, her voice hoarse. 'I'll just need a few minutes to get ready.'

He lifted his coffee cup between them, relaxed now that she'd acquiesced. 'Take your time. I'm going to have this.'

She didn't need long, though. Unlike Cressida, Tilly generally threw on what she had to hand and finger-combed her hair to make it slightly less wild. The most she ever dressed up was on the occasions when she was pretending to be Cressida Wyndham.

She showered, scrubbing her skin until it was pink, then wrapped a towel around her body. She peeked down the hallway, making sure he wasn't nearby, before stepping out of the bathroom. She moved quickly to her room, but just at the second she reached the door he stepped out of his, and his powerful frame connected with hers—hard.

She had the brief impression of his head having been bent, his mind distracted—enough to convince her that it was an accident.

'Ow!' she snapped, forgetting momentarily that beneath the towel she was naked and wet. 'Watch where you're going!'

But he *was* watching. In that moment he was watching every single movement on Tilly's face, seeing so much more than she was aware she was showing. The way her eyes clouded, turning a darker green when they met his. The way her pupils dilated under his watch, spinning into big black orbs. And the way her lips parted, revealing a moist tongue that nervously traced her lower lip.

Rio lifted his hands to her shoulders, his expression dark.

Her breath was rasping and fast. She stared at him, and all thoughts of being strong and keeping him at arm's length fled her mind. Only desire was left.

His eyes probed hers and his fingers on her wet flesh were gently insistent as they stroked. She moaned, low in her throat, and swept her eyes closed.

Without make-up, her skin glowing from the shower, her hair pulled up into a messy bun, and with a tiny towel barely covering her, she was the most desirable woman he had ever seen.

Rio glided his hands over her upper arms, but he wanted more. His hand moved to the back of her towel, pushing her towards him. She connected with his body—by design this time. She was soft and small, her curves fitting perfectly to him, as though they'd been designed for one another.

Her lashes were dark, feathered fans against her flushed cheeks. And the small moan she made sent his pulse into overdrive. Would she moan when they made love? Would her pillowy lips part, breathing those sweet sounds into the air?

His need was a tsunami inside him, crashing inexorably towards land. She was the shore…she was the anchor…and he was powerless to fight the pull of her tide. Rio had never considered himself powerless before. But he didn't care. What did power matter when there was the delight of Cressida Wyndham to be had?

He lifted his hand to her face, cupping her cheek

and sweeping the ball of his thumb over her lower lip. Her eyes flew open, pinning him with a look that held the same tsunami of need that was ravaging his defences.

'We shouldn't do this,' she said quietly, but her hips pushed forward, moving from side to side in an ancient silent invitation.

His fingers moved through her hair, pulling it from the bun, running through the ends. 'We shouldn't,' he agreed darkly.

'I don't…just sleep with guys,' she whispered, closing her eyes on the confession.

And it *was* a confession, he realised. There was guilt and shame in it—as though she had been keeping it a secret. It confused the hell out of him, because he would have put money on Cressida sleeping with pretty much anyone she found attractive.

Curiosity flared and challenge lay before him. Not to sleep with her so much as to find out more about her before he gave in to temptation.

'Do you kiss them?' he asked.

She smiled, but before she could answer his mouth was crushing down on hers. It was a kiss driven by a passion that had burst out of their control; it was its own force, enormous and undeniable. His tongue was fierce in her mouth, and she surrendered to him willingly. She melted against him, her whole body catching fire.

Her hands pushed into his hair. His body was a weight against hers. He moved her easily, pushing her back against the wall. The pressure of his frame kept her standing, his strong legs pinning her on either side, his mouth making her forget anything except this. This moment, this need.

The world seemed to stop. His hands reached lower and it wasn't until they curved over hers that Tilly realised she'd been about to unhook her towel, wanting to lower it, to be naked *for* him and *with* him. His hands held it still, though, and he broke the kiss just enough to look down at her.

'No.' He shook his head, and his expression was so serious that she wondered for a terrifying moment, if she'd mistaken his interest in her. But he'd kissed her? Hadn't he? Or had she kissed him?

Doubt and worry replaced desire, dousing it quickly. 'Oh, I thought…'

'You don't just sleep with men, remember?' he prompted, his breath strained, his chest moving quickly.

Her eyes clouded, almost changing colour as she reached through the strands of memory to recall what he was talking about. 'Oh, right,' she muttered, wishing she could eat those words.

'And if you take this towel off I don't think either of us will be able to stop what was about to happen from happening.'

She nodded, but embarrassment was making it difficult to accept his explanation. Because Tilly didn't want to stop. She wanted to give in to this—them—here and now.

'I am only human, *cara*,' he said gently. 'And already I find I cannot get you out of my mind.'

She drew in a deep breath at the admission. 'Really?'

His laugh came from deep in his throat. 'Really.'

'I thought maybe I was the only one fighting this.'

He shook his head and moved forward again, pinning her with his body so that she could be in no doubt as to how he felt.

'I have been like this since we swam, yesterday.'

Her cheeks suffused with colour. 'Oh…'

He grinned. 'Yes. Oh.'

She bit down on her lip and forced herself to meet his gaze. 'So…?'

'I am not often surprised,' he said, and it was a thick admission. 'But you surprise me. I like that.'

It did little to clear up her feelings, but she nodded. 'I… I guess I'll get dressed, then.'

If Tilly had thought her nerves stretched tight before, they were now at breaking point. A bumpy boat ride to Capri hadn't helped. Nor had the sight of Rio at the helm, his shirtsleeves pushed up to his elbows, exposing tanned forearms and capable hands, his strong body braced as they crested the waves.

By the time they arrived she was parched, and just about ready to beg him to relent, to find some place where they could be together and see if that cured her desperate state of longing.

He pulled the boat directly into a cove, bringing it to a stop beside a wooden jetty. He stood up and tossed out a thick rope, catching a hook which he used to bring the boat in closer. He jumped up, in an impressive display of athleticism, looping the rope several times and then putting a hand down to her.

Tilly eyed it suspiciously, but his smile made her laugh. 'Yeah, okay. I've learned my lesson.'

Still, she was tentative as she reached up and placed her fingers in his palm.

It was like being electrocuted. Her whole body was quivering with it. Her eyes met his helplessly. She was lost.

From what she could tell, Rio was focussed only on getting her out of the boat safely. She climbed up, knowing that she must look ridiculous as she scrambled onto the jetty. She went to thank him and pull away, but he shifted his fingers, lacing them through hers, holding on to her hand.

Emotion caught at her throat.

It was just about the sweetest gesture she'd ever known. A simple touch, an innocent closeness, and yet it filled her with pleasure.

The shore of Capri was dotted with colourful homes built right into the sheer cliff face. Shops and restaurants dotted the shoreline, and in the small bay bright boats bobbed gently on the water.

'What do you need?' she asked, her eyes taking in the picturesque scene.

'Apart from the obvious?' He grinned. 'I have to pick up a few things.'

'That's cryptic,' she teased.

'Uh-huh. That is me. International man of mystery.'

She laughed. 'Okay, mystery man. Where to first?'

The marina at which Rio had moored the boat was small, but a short stroll away there was a market.

It turned out that grocery items seemed to be the sum total of what was required. He paused to pick up a baguette, some tomatoes, olives, oil and cheese. While Rio shopped, Tilly followed, pausing to admire the stalls that caught her attention, wondering at the artful displays and delicious-looking treats.

He paused to speak to a man selling grapes and she spied a little shop across the cobbled path. 'I'm just going to have a look in there,' she murmured, moving away before he could speak.

She slipped inside and breathed in the familiar scent of second-hand books. Dust and imagination swirled around her.

'*Buongiorno.*' the woman behind the counter smiled, her wiry frame shifting forward a little in acknowledgement of Tilly's arrival.

'*Ciao.*'

Tilly disappeared into the shelves, picking up a few titles that interested her before settling near the children's books. The titles were difficult to translate, but the names of the authors were obvious.

At the very bottom, hidden behind a wall of Harry Potter translations, she saw a familiar binding. 'Aha!' She slipped it out. *Il Castello Sulla Scogliera* stared back at her. She had read all the *Famous Five* books as a child. She flicked the pages and ran her finger over the words. A foreign language couldn't diminish the promise of the book.

She moved to the cash register and placed her trophy down, hoping her smile would compensate for the fact that she didn't speak more than a few words of Italian.

The woman nodded, as if understanding, and pointed to the price on the cover. Tilly fumbled into her handbag, bypassing her phone on her way to her wallet. Her phone! She hadn't even realised that here in Capri she must have reception.

She placed a ten euro note on the counter and waited for change. The woman slid the book into a brown paper bag, her smile dismissive.

'*Grazie,*' Tilly murmured, nestling the book into her bag as she lifted her phone. She switched it on and waited for it to load up.

A few text messages came in—one from Jack, thanking her again for saving his life, one from her mother, asking if she was coming for dinner at the weekend, and one from Art asking where a file had been saved on her computer.

She tapped out a quick reply to Art, and then went into her emails. There was nothing from Cressida.

She lifted her gaze, scanning the market, and located Rio instantly. Though he was surrounded by other shoppers, she could have spotted him from five times the distance.

As if sensing her inspection, he looked up, his eyes clashing with hers. The zing of lust was strong enough to make her slow to a stop. It was overwhelming.

He made up for her lack of movement, cutting through the shoppers easily until he was right before her.

'Lunch?' he prompted, his eyes dropping to her lips in a way that made her want to lift her mouth and kiss him.

Wordlessly, she nodded.

Lunch first. And whatever else he wanted after that.

CHAPTER SIX

THE RESTAURANT OVERLOOKED the whole bay. It was up at least a hundred narrow steps, but as Tilly stared over the sweeping ocean, seeing the colourful boats and the golden sun, she admitted to herself that the climb had absolutely been worth it.

Lavender framed the terrace, exploding from terracotta pots, spiking the air with darts of mauve. She reached forward and clipped one of the leaves, lifting it to her nose. The tell-tale scent came to her quickly, but there was something else. She craned forward and beneath the pot plant saw a tiny jasmine vine scrambling up the wall, reaching towards her.

'Do not even *think* about falling,' a dark voice murmured from just behind her.

She straightened, casting a look over her shoulder and rolling her eyes.

But her heart slammed against her ribcage when she saw Rio holding a bottle of wine and two glasses. Her eyes stuck to him, as though glued.

'I have ordered lunch,' he murmured, nodding towards the table directly beside them.

She nodded—a tiny movement.

He poured two glasses of wine; it was ice-cold and

a buttery yellow colour. He lifted one and handed it to her, his eyes holding hers.

'Cheers,' she said as she took it, and he lifted his glass, clinking it against the side of hers lightly. 'Have you been here before?'

'To Capri?'

'No. To this restaurant.'

'Ah. Once, when I first visited Prim'amore.'

Her curiosity over his decision to buy it flared back to life. 'Did you inspect the island like I am?'

'No.' He forced a smile to his face. 'It was a sudden visit.'

'Why?' She sipped her wine automatically and found it to be delicious. Fruity without being cloying, and refreshing.

He angled his face to hers. 'There wasn't time to explore.'

'Are you being deliberately evasive?'

He sipped his wine, his eyes locked to hers over the rim. 'No.'

'So...?'

He expelled a sigh. 'I have spent a lifetime not discussing this.'

Her interest doubled. She waited, holding her breath, for him to continue.

'There is something about you...' He shook his head slowly. 'I inherited the island,' he said after a moment's pause. 'A little over a month ago.'

'Oh.' Sympathy clouded her expression. 'I'm sorry.'

'What for?'

'Well, if someone left you a whole island, you must have meant a lot to them.'

His smile was brief: a flicker of disagreement disguised as a polite acknowledgement. 'I don't want it.'

She mulled over that for a moment. 'Because of Arketà?'

'Because it reminds me of things I would rather forget,' he corrected.

A sound alerted them to someone's approach. Rio straightened, and his air of confiding drifted away.

The waiter placed two plates on their table. One held an assortment of seafood—calamari, prawns, *vongole* and oysters. The other had slices of tomato, white spheres of cheese and marinated artichoke hearts.

Her stomach gave an anticipatory lurch. She was impatient to taste the flavours. But her mind was even more impatient. She wanted to know everything about him.

Apparently she was not alone in her curiosity.

'I misjudged you completely,' he said slowly, thoughtfully, leaning back in his chair and waving a hand over the plates, indicating that she should help herself. 'I thought you would be selfish and boring. Vapid and vain.'

'Gee, thanks,' she snapped, fluttering her lashes to look down at the food. She reached for some calamari and a few pieces of tomato, simply to disguise the guilt on her face.

'I have apologised for this,' he said seriously, his voice deep. 'I meant it. You are not the woman I thought. So who *are* you?'

She swallowed. Despair was a chasm beneath her, trying its hardest to suck her in. What could she tell him? Not a lot. At least not without breaking the promise she'd made to Cressida.

She met his gaze, but her eyes were hesitant. 'What do you want to know?'

He was thoughtful, as though she'd suggested he write a blank cheque and he was appraising how much to make it out for. 'I was under the impression that you were…how should I put this? *Liberal* with your affections?'

She smothered a laugh of indignation. 'Is that a euphemism for being easy to get into bed?'

He shook his head, a rueful smile on his lips. 'I make no judgements. I enjoy sex as much as anyone. I do not care how many partners my lovers have had before me.'

She squeezed her eyes shut. Just the idea of being grouped in with his lovers made her blood simmer painfully inside her. 'How enlightened of you.'

'It is this that fascinates me. This coy embarrassment, your prudish disapproval. As though you have never slept with a man.'

Her lips formed an 'oh' of surprise. 'Just because this morning I said I wasn't in the habit of having sex with random men?'

'Partly.' He sipped his wine, his eyes still appraising her. 'But it is more than that. It is the way you tremble when I touch you—even lightly.'

As if to prove his point, he reached across the table and lifted her hand, pressing a kiss against the sensitive flesh of her inner wrist. To her chagrin, a shiver of awareness flew over her, coating her flesh in goosebumps and warming her core.

The widening of his eyes showed he had seen the effect he had on her. 'Nothing about you adds up.'

Fear stilled her. She was failing. She was letting her own selfish needs get in the way of what she was supposed to be doing. What she'd been paid handsomely to do.

Cressida was counting on her and Tilly had given her word.

She had no right to be jeopardising everything just because she was...falling in love?

Her mouth parted in surprise. Was that what she was doing? It felt so alien to her.

Her heart rocketed in her chest and her mind ran away with her. *Love?* She'd never been in love. Not once. She'd dated some nice guys, and she'd even slept with two of her boyfriends—the ones she'd thought might eventually become serious prospects for Happily Ever After. And there'd been one ill-advised one-night stand that had taught her she didn't go in for casual sex.

But she'd never felt anything remotely like this.

'I'm not an equation,' she mumbled, pulling her hand away and reaching for her wine. 'I'm not something to make sense of.'

'On the contrary, you are a riddle I want to solve.'

She swallowed, her throat knotting visibly as she tried to refresh her parched throat. When that didn't work she lifted her wine to her lips and gulped it gratefully.

She toyed with the collar of her dress. 'Speaking of solving riddles,' she said, in a heavy-handed attempt at changing the subject, 'I have something for you.'

He was quiet, but she sensed his impatience with the roadblock she'd erected. She reached into her handbag and pulled out the book, passing it to him with a shy smile.

He unfolded it, and when he saw the title his confusion grew. 'This is the book you told me of?'

'It's not just a book,' she corrected. 'It's a series. This is one of them. The only one I could find at that little shop.'

She sipped her wine again, surprised to realise the glass was almost empty.

'Thank you,' he murmured, flipping the pages and giving them a cursory inspection before putting it aside. 'Did you read a lot when you were growing up?'

She wasn't fooled for a moment. He seemed to be making casual conversation, but it was all part of his same quest to solve the riddle of who she was—a riddle she'd never be able to answer.

Desolation washed over her. Was there any way she could be honest with him? The idea gnawed at her mind.

She reached for her wine, the idea taking purchase inside her. If she told him the truth, then what? Would he go along with her ruse? Would he still look at her as though he wanted to peel the clothes from her body and make her his? Or would he judge her for engaging in this kind of subterfuge? For taking payment for a lie?

Or what if she could speak to Cressida? What if she confessed the truth to the other woman and asked her to release Tilly from their agreement? She'd have to pay the money back but, given time, she could do that.

Suddenly keeping this secret for the heiress felt all kinds of wrong.

'That does not seem like a complex question,' he prompted.

Her eyes were enormous in her face. 'Huh?'

'Did you read much when you were growing up?'

She pulled a face, doing her best to hide her embarrassment and refocus her attention on their conversation. 'Yes.'

She had lived in the pages of books. Jack, less so.

'And these were your favourites?'

'Amongst my favourites,' she agreed. 'I adored any mystery books. I must have read the same ones a thousand times.'

He reached for the bottle of wine, topping her glass up as he settled back in his chair.

'And you?'

'No, I didn't read.'

'Not at all?' she murmured, finding that almost impossible to comprehend. 'That's so sad.'

He laughed. 'I had other pastimes that I enjoyed very much.'

'Such as?'

'Exploring.' His face flashed with an expression similar to what she imagined he might have worn as a young boy. 'My mother and I would walk—at least we would when she was well enough.'

He stared out at the ocean, a smile crinkling the corners of his eyes as he thought back to those brief windows of happiness in his childhood.

'She didn't have a lot of money, as I have said, so she would pack a bag with apples and water, and a little *cioccolata* for me. We lived above the *mar-*

cato, and every now and again she would surprise me with a fresh-baked pastry or some deli meat. We would leave early in the morning and not return until nightfall. All day we would walk through the winding streets of Rome, studying the ancient buildings, learning about the city.'

He turned his attention back to Tilly.

'I do not consider I missed any advantage because I wasn't an avid fan of books.'

She dipped her head forward and a wisp of red hair brushed against her pale complexion. Tilly had read in order to have exactly the same adventures.

'Those walks sound beautiful,' she said softly. 'Was she sick often?'

His eyes met Tilly's, and again she had the sense that he was waging an internal war. Perhaps it was easy for her to recognise because she was fighting a similar battle. What to show and what to hide.

'Yes.'

It was impossible to flatten the sorrow in her expressive eyes. She reached across the table and curled her hand over his. He stared at their fingers, as did she. Was he noticing the way they fitted together so well? Even the contrast between his deep tan and her cream complexion created a striking image.

'When I started school, I remember her telling me that things would be different. I didn't realise at the time why—only that she seemed buoyed up by the prospect of something on the horizon. With hindsight, I understand. Finally I would be cared for during the week, which would allow her to work. She saw an opportunity to get her life back on track.'

'Do you think her life *wasn't* on track, Rio?' Tilly asked thoughtfully.

He swirled his wine in the glass without drinking it. Having not spoken to a soul about his childhood, he found the combination of sunshine, wine and the beautiful woman opposite like a magical key to the doorway of his past.

'She was twenty-four when I was born,' he murmured, his eyes lifting to Tilly's face. 'Your age.'

She ran her thumb over his hand. 'What did she do? For work, I mean?'

His smile was perfunctory. 'She was an architect.'

Pieces of the jigsaw slipped into place, building a framework as to who he was.

'She taught you to love old buildings,' Tilly murmured thoughtfully.

'Yes. Though it wasn't so much teaching as opening my eyes. Whenever we walked past demolition sites we'd marvel at what might have been done if only someone had intervened. She loved history. The past. She wanted to preserve it.'

'She sounds like a wonderful person.' And a lot like her son, she added silently.

'*Si.*'

He wondered at the way he was opening up to this woman he barely knew—a woman he had thought he would despise. But the more he got to know her, the more he understood Cressida's differences from the Marinas of the world. Cressida didn't have it in her to lie.

'And when did she first get sick?'

His eyes were as hard as flint; they showed no

emotion, but Tilly could feel it vibrating from him in waves.

'A month after I started school. She thought it was a cold, but it wouldn't go away. Then there was stomach pain.'

He closed his eyes for a moment, and when he looked at her once more it was as though he was piercing her with his pain. Tilly felt his trauma as if it was her own.

'She was too sick to work. She lost her job. Money became tighter…she became increasingly ill.'

'Oh, Rio,' Tilly murmured, shaking her head as she contemplated his life. 'What about her parents? Your father?'

'Her parents didn't speak to her from the moment they discovered she was pregnant.'

'Not even when you were born?' Tilly demanded, aghast and outraged in equal measure.

His expression was sardonic. 'Not when I was born. Not when she got sick. Not even when she died—though they are both alive to this day.'

'And do you speak to them?'

He shot her a look of impatience. 'Would *you*?'

Her heart flipped painfully.

She searched for something to say—something that might alleviate his suffering—but he continued, 'I do not believe in second chances, Cressida. We have one opportunity in life to make the right choice. They did not. Nor did my father. Forgiving them would be a sign of stupidity—a weakness I will never allow myself to possess.'

The words were spoken with such passion that she couldn't help but comprehend the depths of his commitment. But the philosophy itself…? It spread panic over her—and not just because she feared her deceit was something else he would not forgive.

'But what if they regret what they did? What if—?'

'No.'

He slashed his free hand through the air and her nerves quivered.

'No,' he softened it, bringing that same hand to rest on hers, sandwiching it between his palms. 'If you can imagine the way she lived her life—the shame she felt at our poverty, the worry she felt when I complained that I was hungry…'

His eyes met Tilly's and the strength of burning emotion made her want to say or do something—anything to erase his pain.

'I was always hungry.' He gave a short, sharp laugh.

'You were a growing boy.'

'And she was a dying woman,' he said softly. 'She stayed alive until I was almost finished at high school, and I believe that was through determination alone.'

He pulled his hands away, reaching for his fork and spearing a sphere of *bocconcini*.

She didn't see him eat it. She was imagining this proud, strong man as he'd been back then. 'What about your father?'

He forked a piece of calamari. 'What about him?'

'You said he's not in the picture,' she prompted. 'But surely when she got sick…?'

'No.'

Her brows knitted together. 'Did he know?'

He flicked her a look of subdued amusement. *'Si, cara.'*

'Perhaps he wasn't in a position to help,' she suggested, finding it impossible to reconcile the idea of a man turning his back on the dying mother of his child.

Rio's eyes narrowed and he was a businessman again. One capable of eviscerating his foes without breaking a sweat. 'Why are you so determined to see the best in people?'

She sipped her wine nervously. 'I don't know. I didn't know that was something I do.'

He nodded curtly. 'You do. And I would think you've had enough experience with people and their selfish proclivities to adopt a more cautious attitude.'

'No.' She shook her head. 'Not yet.'

He lifted one dark, thick brow. 'I hope you do not change,' he said quietly. 'Your optimism is refreshing.'

'But misplaced?' she suggested.

'Yes—in this instance. My father was a very wealthy man. He could have bought my mother an apartment, given her an allowance and ensured I went to excellent schools. It would have been barely small change to him.'

'Surely he did *something* to help?'

His laugh was a dark sound. 'He offered to pay for the termination.'

Tilly's gasp was loud. There was one other couple in their corner of the terrace and they turned towards them, apparently curious at what was going on.

With an effort at discretion, she said more quietly, 'Are you sure? Are you absolutely sure?'

Though she didn't want to suggest it of the woman he obviously viewed as a saint, it wasn't inconceivable that his mother had lied at some stage, to sour Rio against the father he'd never met.

As if he'd read her mind, he said, 'My mother never told me. At least, she didn't mean to. But there were times when her pain was so severe that her doctors put her on huge quantities of morphine. It made her…communicative.'

Tilly grimaced. 'That's rough on your mother. To have kept a brave face through so much adversity, raising you without badmouthing your father, no matter how sorely she was tempted, only to find the confession escaping without her control. How invasive.'

His eyes showed surprise at her perception. 'That is exactly how I feel. I would never have confronted her with what she'd said. Seeing her experience guilt for telling me would have been mortifying. Worse, if she'd tried to apologise. In any event, I was glad to have answers. I had always wondered about him. I was relieved to discover that I could hate him. That I was right to feel that. It had been in me for a long time, but we are taught not to hate our parents, no? I felt vindicated.'

She nodded, but knew there was nothing she could say to relieve his pain. It must be a pain akin to death.

'Is he still alive?'

'No.'

She reached for her wine and lifted it towards her lips without drinking. 'I don't know what to say.'

A muscle jerked in his square jaw. 'You are the only person I have ever spoken to about this. It is enough that you have listened.'

Was it wrong to feel such delight in a moment of sadness? Tilly did. Her heart soared. He had confided in her—and confided something that he had never shared with another soul.

'I imagine your mother would be very proud of you.' To Tilly's mortification, she found herself choked by the words.

He shrugged. 'She always was.'

His eyes met hers, and she couldn't have looked away for a million pounds. She was trapped in his gaze and there was nowhere else she wanted to be.

'Even my smallest feats attracted an improbable amount of praise.' He was amused—or perhaps aiming to lighten the tone.

'My mother is like that,' Tilly said, thinking of Belinda Morgan with an indulgent smile. 'If I won a spelling competition at school it was like an Olympic Gold to her.'

His expression was watchful. Almost calculating. Tilly didn't realise why at first, but a moment later it dawned on her. Cressida's mother was nothing like Belinda, and she had certainly never been proud of her daughter.

'I see.'

Tilly panicked for a moment, wondering if he really did. She needed to regroup urgently. She needed to speak to Cressida.

'Would you excuse me a moment?'

He nodded and she stood, scooping up her bag as she made her way across the terrace and back into the restaurant. She pushed inside the restroom and lifted her phone out of her bag, dialled Cressida's number.

It went straight to voicemail.

She tried again—without success.

Tilly stared at herself in the mirror for a moment, studying her face, bracing her hands on the counter.

She'd promised Cressida she'd help, and generally she wouldn't even think of letting someone down. But she'd never known a man like Rio before, and the sense that she would stuff everything up if she kept lying to him was like a snake tightening around her chest.

She tapped out a quick message to Cressida.

We need to talk. I have limited email access. Please get in touch.

She made her way back to the table, her mind over-flowing with erratic, confused thoughts as she eased herself back into the seat.

'You said you've known lots of women like me?'

It was out of left field, but he caught her drift immediately. 'And then I said you are unique.'

The hair on the back of her neck stood on end. Pleasure was dancing through her.

'You have an active social life?' she asked, moving back to her original subject.

He seemed to allow the shift, and she was utterly relieved. She reached for her wine and drank thirstily. But when she placed the glass back on the table she felt woozy. She had barely eaten, she chastised herself inwardly, reaching for a piece of cheese and popping it in her mouth.

He was watching her. More specifically, he was watching her lips. Her mouth.

He picked another piece of cheese off the plate and lifted it to her lips, brushing it across them, waiting, watching. She parted her mouth just enough and he pushed it inside. His thumb stayed at the corner of her lip and she chewed, but her heart was like thunder in her breast.

'Yes.'

Confusion swirled inside her. 'Yes, what?'

'Yes, I have an active social life. I presume that's a coy way of referring to my sex life?'

More wine. No. More food. Her wine glass was empty anyway. She needed water. She looked around, searching for a waiter. There were none nearby.

She nodded. It was a confession she might never have made if it hadn't been for the two decent-sized glasses of Pinot Grigio she'd just consumed in rapid succession and on an empty stomach.

'Have you ever been serious about anyone?' she asked, the question escaping as if blurted out by accident.

His eyes shimmered with an emotion she didn't comprehend. *'Si.'*

Jealousy fired in her soul.

'Really?'

He nodded. 'A long time ago.'

'What happened?'

His laugh was light-hearted enough. 'She broke my heart.'

'Really?'

'No, *cara.* Not really. At the time she betrayed me I was angry. I thought I might be falling in love with her.' He shook his head, his smile natural. 'I wasn't. I couldn't have been. Everything she was turned out to be a lie.'

Acid was bubbling down Tilly's spine. She stared at him with a sense of deep panic.

Everything she was turned out to be a lie.

'A lie how?'

He shook his head. 'It doesn't matter.'

'You're still upset? Too upset to talk about it?'

'No, it just serves no purpose,' he said with a shrug. 'I have learned again and again that people who lie don't get second chances.'

'How did she lie to you?' Tilly pushed, her heart hammering painfully in her chest, guilt at her own deception becoming a maze she needed to find her way out of.

'You really want to know?'

Tilly nodded, but panic was weighing her down.

'We had been seeing each other for nearly a year. I was busy. My business was taking off and, while I liked her, and even thought myself on the way to being in love with her, I had no real plans for her to be a serious or permanent part of my life.'

He looked towards the ocean, catching the glistening sun as it bounced off the sea.

'Marina perhaps began to sense this and, concerned, took matters into her own hands.'

'How?'

His smile was grim. 'By faking a pregnancy.'

Tilly froze, the look on her face pure shock. 'She did what?'

'Mmm…' he agreed. 'Very poor form, no?'

'Absolutely.'

'She knew I would propose. And I would have. But too much didn't add up and eventually she confessed. She was very apologetic—and I understood, to some extent. Marina grew up with everything she ever wanted landing in her lap. She wanted *me*, and my reluctance to commit was not something she was willing to accept.'

'But to lie about being pregnant...' Tilly said angrily.

'*Si*. It was very foolish. I ended our relationship the day I found out and I have not spoken to her since.' His look was loaded with dark emotion. 'I do not invite betrayal twice.'

A shiver ran down her spine and her own predicament swirled through her like a raging tsunami. The imperative to get through to Cressida was growing by the moment, suffocating her with urgency. She had to fix this somehow.

'I don't like to think about you with other women,' she said, but the words were difficult to find in her brain and they came out sounding forced and strange.

She didn't miss the look of intense speculation on his face. 'Jealous?'

Tilly was more than jealous. She was...*devastated*.

She needed time and space to process this. She sipped the wine he'd topped up automatically, desperate to blot the pain from her mind.

'It's not like *my* social life is quiet.'

'And, again, when you say "social life" you mean sex life?' he clarified.

She was Cressida—in that moment, at least.

'Sure. Yeah. You know—sex is sex,' she said, with an attempt at a blasé flick of her wrist. 'Speaking of which...' She leaned forward, placing her hand over his. 'Can we go back to the island now?'

His eyes lanced her. But when he stood and took her hand it was with pure, sensual determination.

This was happening.

CHAPTER SEVEN

'THIS ISN'T GOING to happen.'

Tilly stared at him, her mind foggy. The afternoon sun was bright overhead. In fact it was sultry, and the air was thick. The boat lurched as he pulled it towards Prim'amore, slowing to meet the shore.

'What?'

He stared pointedly at her hand. Without her permission, it had landed on his thigh. No—half on his thigh and embarrassingly close to his arousal.

Wine had made her slow; her mind lagged. 'I…'

'You're drunk,' he said darkly, and with such arrogant disbelief that she was spurred into denying the accusation.

'I am absolutely not,' she snapped, standing up to prove the point.

The boat rocked and, just like the first day they'd met, she began to topple forward. With a muttered curse he caught her, holding her tight around the arms.

'And you are trouble,' he said, without a hint of the affection that had warmed her over lunch.

'*You* are,' she retorted childishly.

'Sit.'

'"Sit",' she mimicked, but she did as he'd said, planting herself back on the seat.

He returned his concentration to the boat, driving it close to the sand and then jumping easily over the front. He used his hands to guide it to the shore and she leaned over the edge, watching him and studying the water at the same time. A school of fish swam beneath them.

The boat thudded as he rolled the tip of it onto the sand before coming around to her side. He held a hand up to Tilly but she stared at it mutinously.

'I can manage.'

He made a derisive noise. 'I've heard that before. Take my hand.'

'No way. Not until you apologise for calling me drunk.' Her demand was somewhat ruined by the hiccough that sliced the sentence in half.

'You had *two* glasses of wine. How can you possibly be intoxicated?' he asked in exasperation.

'I don't...' *Don't drink very often.* The admission died on her lips. 'I don't know,' she finished lamely. 'And I'm fine, thank you very much.'

'Like hell you are,' he snapped. 'Let me help you.'

'You think I'm going to drown in two inches of water?'

'If anyone's capable of it...'

She poked her tongue out and moved to the other side of the boat. He was quick, but she had the advantage, for Rio had water to wade through before he could reach her. She stepped out, nailing the landing.

It was the pirouette that she made in order to gloat that undid her.

She knocked her hip on the edge of the boat and

it jolted her backwards—into the water. A brief recognition of his angry expression was the last thing
she saw before landing in the water.

Again.

She spluttered, pushing up onto her elbows, but
Rio was there, lifting her out of the ocean and hoist-
ing her over his shoulder.

'Put me down!' she said crossly, but she didn't try
to wriggle out of his grip. Not when her hands were
dangling over his curved rear. Curiously, she let her
fingers move towards his waistband, separating it
from his shirt until she found skin.

'And let you fall into a hole or be eaten by a crab?
No, Cressida. I think you need to be chained to a bed
for a while.'

The image was startling. She froze and he let out a
noise from deep in his throat. 'Or a chair. Anywhere
out of harm's way.'

'I like the bed idea…'

He mounted the steps and kicked the door open,
carrying her through the hallway and depositing her
unceremoniously so that she was sitting at the kitchen
bench.

'Do not even *think* about moving,' he said, with
such determination that she was pretty sure the smart
thing to do was what he said.

As soon as the front door slammed shut again she
wriggled off the bench. Stars flashed in her eyes and
she steadied herself by pressing against the fridge.
Water. She needed water.

But she was already wet.

She needed to not be wet.

She swore angrily, mentally shaking herself.

Get changed, then drink something.

She nodded.

It was an excellent plan.

Only Rio wasn't gone long, and her fingers were fumbling too much to perform anything efficiently.

When he walked back into the cottage and found the kitchen deserted, he checked her room.

The door was wide open, and standing by the window was Tilly, in the process of pulling a dry dress on. He saw a glimpse of her naked back, her curved bottom and pale hips. Enough to fuel his fantasies for years to come, he thought grimly.

'*Dio*...' he groaned.

She spun around, and had he been looking at her face he would have seen how unexpected his intrusion was. But his eyes were trained on the body that he'd just caught a tantalising glimpse of, and he possessed her with his gaze when he didn't dare touch her.

Her fingers dropped to the hem of her dress, lifting it, her eyes trained on his, her meaning clear. If he didn't act quickly she was going to be naked again, and he sure as hell wouldn't make any promises about how he'd respond to that.

'I told you,' he said with grim determination. 'This is not going to happen.'

It didn't make sense. He felt it too; she knew he did. He wanted her. 'But I...'

'You can barely stand up, Cressida. Do you think I am the kind of man who would take advantage of a woman so inebriated?'

Alcohol had apparently robbed her of any inhibitions. She walked towards him, her curves hypnotising him as she moved.

'How about letting an inebriated woman take advantage of you?' she suggested quietly, wrapping her arms around his neck, lifting her body higher, pressing her soft round breasts to his torso. 'I want this to happen. Sober or not, I want this.'

He closed his eyes for a moment and then stepped backwards. 'Well, I do not. Especially not like this.'

His words cut her to the quick. Even alcohol couldn't dull the throb of pain.

'Oh.'

He expelled a long, slow sigh, as if taming himself while subduing her. 'Lie down,' he commanded in a dictatorial tone that was softened by a small smile. 'You'll feel like hell in a few hours.'

'I need water,' she said belligerently.

'I'll bring it.'

She didn't thank him, even though she knew she ought to. She practically stomped to the bed and lay down, not bothering to pull the covers back.

She was asleep when he returned a minute later, glass of water in hand. He placed it quietly on the bedside table then left her in peace—before his will-power finally deserted him.

He deserved a bloody medal of valour for that act of self-torture.

After a month of celibacy a gorgeous woman offered her beautiful, perfect self on a platter and he walked away? Hell, it was two glasses of wine—not even half a bottle. How many times had he slept with a woman who'd drunk champagne at a party?

But she hadn't just had two glasses of wine. Or rather, she *had*, but they'd had the effect he would have expected two *bottles* to have. She'd been completely addled. Cressida Wyndham, he had been led to believe, was a sophisticated woman who moved in socially elite circles. A couple of glasses of wine over lunch should not have affected her like that. And yet undeniably they had.

The moment they'd stood up from the table he'd realised that she was no longer herself. It had become more apparent as they'd made their way through the marina and he'd practically had to carry her past the shops. Then there had been the boat ride. The way she'd stroked his thigh the whole way. He'd been tempted to throw the thing into neutral and make love to her then and there.

Had she *any* idea how much stamina it had taken to turn her down?

And what had happened to make her so utterly affected by the wine?

He added that question to the pile of things that simply didn't make sense.

Cressida Wyndham was a mystery. And he was going to solve her.

He'd been right.

She felt awful when she woke. Not least of all because of the sense of temporal disorientation that had made her jerk awake. It was dark, but it didn't feel like the middle of the night. She reached for her phone, pressing the button so that she could see the time.

It was just after nine o'clock.

Why was she asleep so early?

And what was that furry feeling in her mouth?

And just like that it all came flooding back to her.

'Oh, God.' She squeezed her eyes shut.

Embarrassment curdled her blood. She screwed her eyes up tight, but that only made it worse. With her eyes closed, the whole day played out like a movie reel. She'd fallen in the water. Again! And... Her skin burned. She'd practically begged him to make love to her. And he'd told her he wasn't interested!

Tilly jerked her head around, her eyes landing on the glass of water. She lifted it up and drank from it quickly.

The only problem was that then she needed to use the restroom.

And that meant leaving her bedroom and possibly facing him.

She could hold it.

Or not.

She stood up and tiptoed towards the door. The handle was an old Bakelite one and she turned it slowly, so slowly, wincing as it creaked a little. She kept her eyes shut as she pulled the door inwards and then poked her head out quickly.

Left, right—he was nowhere in sight.

Phew.

She practically ran to the bathroom. She felt as fresh as a ten-year-old toothbrush, and a cursory inspection in the mirror showed she looked little better.

She ran her fingers through her hair and splashed water on her face, pinching her cheeks before brushing her teeth and rubbing in face cream. Her skin was warm, perhaps from the sun...or embarrassment. With a grimace, she pulled the door inwards, forgetting to be quiet.

It wouldn't have mattered anyway. Rio was lounging against the wall opposite, his lips twisted in the hint of a knowing smile.

'Don't,' she said quietly, her eyes dropping to the floor. 'Don't lecture me.'

His voice was thick when he spoke. 'I have no intention of it,' he promised. 'How do you feel?'

'How do you think?' she whispered.

He reached out for her hand but she stepped backwards. 'Please, don't,' she said softly. 'I...' What? What could she say? 'I just want to forget today ever happened.'

'I'm sorry to say that is not possible. At least, not for me.'

She groaned, mortification chewing through her.

'Come and eat something.'

'No, thank you.'

'You will feel better in the morning if you go to bed with food in your stomach.'

'Please,' she said sharply. 'It was two glasses of wine. I'm hardly hungover. I just need privacy.'

His eyes narrowed. 'Eat something and I will leave you alone.'

'Are you bribing me with food?'

He shrugged. 'It is your choice.'

Her stomach twisted. She *was* actually hungry. 'Okay,' she said ungratefully. 'Fine.'

He turned on his heel and walked towards the front of the cabin, holding the door open for her.

The night was as balmy as it was beautiful. A thick blanket of stars danced overhead, and the sky was as dark as an inkpot. Streaks of cloud ran like frail fingers towards the moon.

'Here.' He handed her a plate and she looked at it with an unimpressed frown.

'Crackers?'

'Just something light.'

She wrinkled her nose but, truth be told, she wasn't sure she could stomach anything else. She sat down and curled her knees under her chin, biting into a biscuit while her eyes roamed the ocean.

She ate, and silence surrounded them but for the occasional sound of a night bird and the throbbing of the ocean. Once the plate was emptied, she stood again.

'I'm going to bed. Unless you have any objections?'

'Not a one,' he replied. 'Sweet dreams, *cara*.'

The words followed her all the way down the hallway, mocking her.

She'd have sweet dreams, all right, and they both knew who'd be starring in them.

The air smelled different when she woke.

The light had changed too.

Her room felt thick and damp. She turned over in bed, angling her body towards the window. It had blown open during the night and mist had burst in, wrapping around her.

'Lightning,' she said to herself, sitting up and rubbing her eyes.

It was raining heavily, the sound of it falling on the roof adding to the depth of the ocean's thunder. A tremor of emotion built inside of her. Thunderstorms had always stirred strong feelings in her, even as a girl.

She pushed the sheets off and stood, pacing across to the window and standing on tiptoe to see out. The geraniums were in disarray, their blooms drooping indignantly, covered in water. She reached out and flicked at one reassuringly, sending droplets of water scurrying.

The beach looked entirely different. The sand was grey, not white, and the waves were leaden, topped with angry white curls of temper as they hammered against the beach. The sky was steel-like, brightened only by the brief flash of lightning, and then a roll of thunder rattled past her.

Even in her sleep she'd been dreading facing the music with Rio. The weather was heightening the drama of that confrontation. She checked herself in the mirror, pinching her cheeks for colour and brushing her hair so that it was slightly less wild, then skimmed her eyes over her phone to check the time.

It was still early.

Perhaps he wouldn't yet be awake?

The thought of a strong black coffee before she had to see him was cause for optimism.

What would she say?

Memories of how she'd behaved almost made her groan aloud. She'd been rude, provocative, flirtatious, demanding...*drunk*.

Embarrassment made her skin crawl. Sucking in a deep breath of storm-soaked air, she made her way quietly to the kitchen.

'*Buongiorno,*' he said quietly, his eyes appraising her from where he stood, looking impossibly virile and unforgivably *not* hungover.

He had a coffee cup in one hand, and was wearing

only a pair of shorts. A swirl of desire almost drove the mortification from her mind.

'Hi.' She cleared her throat, eyeing the coffee machine and realising she'd have to perform penance first. 'I'm...sorry. About yesterday.'

He arched a brow, and she couldn't tell from his expression if he was still angry. Out of nowhere she saw his face as it had been when she'd fallen in the water. He'd been furious with her.

Tilly dropped her eyes, staring at her brightly painted toenails with earnest concentration.

'I think it was because I hadn't eaten breakfast,' she said quietly. 'And it was hot...and I was thirsty. I just drank too fast,' she finished weakly.

He made a noise of agreement. 'Do you do that often?'

Her eyes were wide. Torn between playing Cressida and defending Tilly, she couldn't say what she wanted. Cressida was practically a professional drinker—and goodness knew what else she indulged in when the party spirit took her.

Tilly shook her head. 'I'm sorry,' she said again, shrugging her shoulders, deciding to stick as close to the truth as possible. 'I'm so embarrassed.'

He strode across the kitchen, putting a hand briefly under her chin so that her face was lifted towards his. 'I do not care that you enjoyed too much wine. I care that you made yourself vulnerable. I care that you exposed yourself to danger. I care that you probably do that often and that any number of men would have revelled in what you offered. You *begged* me to sleep with you, Cressida. How many times have you done that? How many men have taken advantage of you in that state?'

He swore angrily and moved away again, towards the coffee machine. He slid a pod into it and pressed the button, watching as it burst into life.

Tilly couldn't look at him. She stared straight ahead. 'I can take care of myself,' she said quietly.

'I don't believe that.'

He pulled the cup out and handed it to her. She caught its aroma with a stomach-flip of relief. Coffee. Essential. She sipped it quickly, enjoying the pain when it scalded her throat.

'Thank you for last night,' she said softly, changing the subject. 'For not…not…'

His eyes were mocking as they trailed over her body, but he said nothing.

The silence stretched between them, punctuated by the sharp crack of lightning and the rattling of the windows. She curled her fingers more tightly around her coffee cup.

'As tempting as I found you,' he said, and the words were a thick admission, 'I would not have forgiven myself.'

She sipped her coffee, tasting the sweet balm with relief. She should have been grateful for his chivalry, but she felt empty inside. Her longing was enormous and it had been ignored.

'We will be stuck in the house today,' he said. 'The storm is setting in.'

'It's pretty intense,' she agreed, moving towards the windows at the back of the house and peering out, pretending she wasn't still awash with mortification at the scene she'd made the night before. 'Are storms like this common?'

'No. Very rare,' he responded, propping his hip against the kitchen bench.

'You think it'll be like this all day?' She turned to face him and her heart gave a little lurch.

'*Si*. At least.' He crossed the room, pausing beside her, following her gaze. 'We just have to wait it out.'

Just what she needed. To be locked in a tiny house with the man she'd begged to make love to her the night before.

Her smile was weak. 'Great.'

CHAPTER EIGHT

TILLY WAS GOING to burst.

Besides the lashing of the rain and the bursting of thunder the house was silent, and had been all morning. He'd worked, and she'd read—or pretended to read. All she'd been able to do was replay the mortifying moments of the previous day, cringing inwardly as she remembered each little bit of information.

Had she actually been *stroking* him when they were on their way back?

Her cheeks flushed pink. She would never forgive herself. And she'd sure as hell never touch wine again.

She shifted on the couch, curling her legs beneath her and flicking a page.

He had been the perfect gentleman. Was that surprising?

No.

It wasn't.

It was Rio.

Well, so far as impersonating Cressida went she'd nailed it. At least that was some consolation.

He hadn't said a word. And nor had she—though curiosity over what he was doing had begun to fill her, distracting her from the book.

Finally she set it in her lap, her eyes lifting to him.

'Yes?' he murmured, without looking up.

Embarrassment flushed through her once more. She felt like a naughty child caught snacking from the cookie jar. 'Nothing.' She bit down on her lip. 'What are you working on?'

He turned to face her now, his eyes like granite in his handsome face. 'Evaluations.'

'For insurance?'

'No. For purchase.' He pushed back from the table a little, stretching his arms above his head.

Tilly nodded, but she wasn't really thinking about his work. Before she could find another topic a sharp, bright burst of lightning cracked overhead, and was followed immediately by the rumbling of angry thunder so loud that the windows shook. And then the lights began to flicker, before going off completely, plunging them into an eerie semi-darkness.

Though it was the middle of the day, the island was wrapped in grey, the sky thick and unyielding, the sun nowhere to be seen. The cabin almost glowed.

'What happened?' she murmured, standing up instinctively.

He frowned. 'My guess is the generator blew a fuse.'

She blinked. 'Something you can fix?'

'Sure.' He scraped his chair back and moved to the window, peering around the corner of the cabin. 'I'll take a look.'

He'd pulled on a shirt at some point, and now he slipped his shoes on and pushed out through the front door. Curious, she followed—though she stopped on the deck and moved to the side, so she could see him without getting wet.

The generator was apparently round at the side of the house. She peeked around the wall, and more specifically at him. Rain was lashing against him; he was saturated. His clothes were plastered to his body, his hair a dark pelt against his head. He moved confidently, his fingers testing the switches in a box.

He shook his head, his eyes scanning the house before resting on her. 'It's the generator.'

She nodded. Wasn't that what he'd said he'd fix?

He moved closer, standing just beneath her and shouting so she could hear him above the aggressive storm. 'The generator is over there.' He nodded towards a small structure she hadn't noticed before. 'There's a key in the kitchen. Would you get it?'

'Yes. Where?'

'In the drawer with the cutlery.'

She nodded, already moving back into the house. She located it easily and jogged back to the deck. But instead of handing it to him she skipped down the steps. The rain hit her like a wall. Within seconds she was as saturated as he.

He swore under his breath. 'What are you *doing*?'

'Helping.' She handed him the key and he took it with a small shake of his head.

'Go inside! I don't need help.'

She compressed her lips and turned her back on him. She didn't go inside, though. She picked her way over the muddy ground, towards the timber construction he'd indicated.

She waited for him, so wet that she barely felt the

rain now. But it was still hammering into her, enormous drops falling thick and fast.

'Fine.' He spoke loudly, but she still had to lean forward to catch his words. 'Seeing as you're here, hold the door open for me.'

He crouched down and unlocked a padlock, then pushed at the slatted door. She hooked her fingers over the top and pulled it wide, holding it even as the wind grew and tried to pull it away from her.

He leaned further into the box, his hands pushing at various things, and Tilly wondered how the heck he knew what he was doing. Or maybe he didn't, and he was going to break the generator and they'd have to leave the island.

The idea pulled at her in a strange way. She hadn't wanted to come away for a week, and yet now, four days in, she couldn't bear the thought of leaving. Was that all it took? Four days? Four days to become so hooked on someone that the idea of waking up without knowing you were going to see them filled you with despair?

He stood up again, pulling the door out of her grip and slamming it shut. He locked it and then nodded towards the house.

He didn't speak until they were on the deck, drenched and dripping. The rain was just as loud there, though, the roof doing little to block out the sound.

'Something's fried it. Could have been the lightning. Could have been an animal running scared. I've rebooted it, so with any luck it will be on again in a few hours.'

A shiver ran down her spine. 'And if it's not?'

'We're stuck here until the storm passes. We will just have to make do.'

Stuck here. In a dark cabin. With Rio. All she needed was candles and music and she'd be about ready to step straight into fantasy.

'There are some candles in the bathroom,' he said, thinking aloud, his eyes scanning her face. 'You need to get dry.'

'So do you,' she pointed out belligerently.

'You are shivering.'

'I know.' She nodded, her teeth chattering together.

'Go. Get dry.'

'What are you going to do?' she asked.

'Check the perimeter,' he shouted, as another flash of lightning slammed through the air around them. 'Make sure the roof is secure.'

'Then I'm coming with you.'

'*Dio!* For once can you just *not* argue with me?'

She crossed her arms. 'Which way?'

'No!' He reached for the door of the cabin and held it open, waiting for her to go inside.

But Tilly was stubborn—especially when she was right. And even more so when she was in love.

'I will work quicker if I am not making sure you don't fall over or bang your head. Go inside.'

She stared at him, her temper spiking. Sure, she was accident-prone, but he didn't need to be so unkind about it!

The memory of the day before—the way she'd crashed out of the boat and into the water—was at the top of her mind.

'I want to help,' she said loudly, but the words were uncertain.

'Then go inside. I will be five minutes.'

She glared at him angrily, her chin tilted defiantly. 'Unless you physically push me inside, then I'm going to follow you.'

He muttered something under his breath—something she didn't quite catch.

'What?'

'I said, don't tempt me!'

Thunder crashed, breathing urgency into the situation. Apparently thinking better of arguing with her, he shook his head and stormed off down the steps. She followed, bracing herself for the rain a microsecond before it began to hammer against her head.

Rio was so fit—so strong. She marvelled at the way he reached up and pushed at the windows, then overturned an old crate and stood on it, pushing a thick piece of wood into the gutter and freeing clogged leaves. He moved around the back of the cabin then, still checking windows.

When they'd almost looped back to the front, he sent her a look that was fulminating with anger. Tilly didn't understand it—though that was perhaps because she hadn't realised that her skin was white and her teeth were shaking in her mouth as she shivered unstoppably.

He stood abruptly and moved towards her, putting a hand in the small of her back and propelling her towards the deck. She turned to face him, but one look at his profile kept her silent.

At least it did until they were on the deck, with the rain lashing in sideways.

'What is it?' she shouted. 'Why do you seem so angry with me?'

'Angry with you?' He pulled the door to the cabin inwards. 'You think I'm *angry* with you?'

'You're shouting at me!' she yelled back. 'Why?'

He shook his head; water droplets fanned out, splashing against the walls. 'Because!'

'That's not an answer. What *is* it? I've already… I said I was sorry about yesterday.'

He closed his eyes for a second, and when he opened them she felt as if he was trying to get a grip on his temper. His eyes were a storm that raged as intensely as the one outside. He swore sharply— a sound that tore through the house as he moved towards her quickly, crushing her body with his far bigger one, pushing her back until she connected with the wall.

His kiss had the strength of an ocean. His tongue drove into her mouth, clashing with hers, his hands pushed at her shoulders and his legs kept her pinned to the wall.

'I am not angry with you, *cara*,' he muttered into her mouth.

The words came to her from a long way away. Her senses weren't capable of absorbing anything but this—this feeling that was tearing her body apart with a need she had never known possible.

Her fingers pushed at his wet clothes; they stuck to his body stubbornly and she groaned into his mouth, pushing her body forward, needing closeness, wanting more. So badly wanting more.

He had far more success—tearing the dress over her head, breaking the kiss for the smallest moment possible in order to shift the fabric over her face. Her mouth chased him, seeking him, needing him, hating his absence. Her pulse was louder even than the thunderstorm.

His hands ran over her sides and she shivered.

'You're cold,' he said, lifting his head.

She shook her head. 'No.'

'You are covered in goosebumps,' he pointed out thickly, the words dragged from him.

'Not cold.' She shook her head and pulled at his shirt, bringing him back to her.

His kiss was everything that had been building up inside her since she'd arrived on Prim'amore. It was all the longing and wanting, the needing and watching. It swirled around them both, churning them, changing everything.

Her fingers tangled in his hair and he groaned into her mouth—a guttural sound that perfectly expressed what she wanted. He pushed at her, guiding her, pulling her, until she was through the door to her bedroom. But he didn't stop. His body kept pushing at hers until she fell backwards onto the bed, a tangle of limbs and desire.

His mouth on hers was demanding; she gave him everything. But then he moved, dragged his stubbled jaw down her body, pushing at her bra so that he could take a nipple in his mouth.

His tongue flicked at it relentlessly, and the pleasure was so intense it was almost too much. She cried out, her hands needing to touch him, to feel him. She pushed at his shirt and finally he paused, so that he could remove it for her. She drove her nails along his back, feeling his supple skin as he turned his attention to her other breast, his fingers picking up where his mouth had left off. She arched her back as pleasure throbbed hard in her abdomen.

'I am not angry with you,' he said again, though she was no longer worried he was.

She nodded, words failing her. He brought his mouth to hers and his kiss was gentle. Slow. Deep. As if he could taste her soul and wanted to cherish her.

It was the most erotic thing she'd ever felt.

'Rio…' she whispered, her skin flushed, her heart thumping.

Rain lashed at the window and lightning struck, but it was mute to them. Only the thundering of their own need registered. He kicked at his trousers; they didn't move easily. He stood, his eyes pinning her, his hands pushing at his clothes so that finally he was naked.

And spectacular.

Tilly stared at him, her eyes hungry for his nakedness, her body needing him. And he understood that need for it was eating him alive too.

He bent forward and pulled at her underpants, but he forced himself to move slowly, to drag them from her with a tantalising, torturous thoroughness, his hands grazing her legs as he went. Legs that were quivering with need.

Impatient, she pushed onto her elbows, but he was standing again, his eyes running over her with such obvious hunger that her whole body flushed.

'You are perfect, Cressida.'

The sentiment was beautiful, but how it pained Tilly to hear another woman's name on his lips at this moment.

'Call me *cara*,' she said, forcing a smile to her lips. 'I like it when you do that.'

'Then it is what I will always call you…*cara*.'

Always? She liked the sound of that.

'You are sure about this?' he asked, reaching down and stroking her face.

She nodded. She was. She absolutely was.

His laugh was uneven. 'Good.'

Then he stood once more and shook his head.

'A moment.'

When he returned, it was with a foil wrapper.

'I nearly forgot,' Tilly whispered, her eyes wide.

'You and me both.' He opened it and sheathed himself, then brought his body over hers. 'I have wanted you from the first moment I saw you,' he said seriously. 'You have a power over me…'

Her heart squeezed in her chest.

It was the same for her.

Except it was a lie.

Everything she was turned out to be a lie.

He'd been burned by a lover in the past, and the last thing Tilly wanted was for that betrayal to colour what they were. Because her name didn't matter, did it?

She shook her head and reached for him. Of course it didn't. This wasn't a lie. What her name was didn't matter—nor what he thought it to be. This thing between them had nothing to do with a name. It was inevitable and it was *them*. Him…her. Their bones, blood, hearts and souls.

His weight was heaven. His body was warmth. He kissed her—gently at first, and then with desperation as his manhood moved towards her, nudging her entrance slowly, gently, cautiously.

Waiting was agony; her body was on fire and only he could douse the flames. She arched her back, lifting herself higher, inviting him wordlessly inside her, and he groaned as he thrust deep, stretching her muscles, plunging to the core of her being.

She cried out in ecstasy, throwing her head back and banging it on the timber wall. He reached up, concern on his features, but she laughed.

'*Maldestra...*' he whispered, and the word ran over her skin.

She didn't know what it meant, and she had no time to ask. He gripped her hips and pulled her lower on the bed, then thrust into her again, sending her body into a spasm of awareness that travelled through her.

A low murmuring was filling the room; it was *her*. Tilly was crying out, over and over and over, indecipherable words, simply needing to express what was happening to her. She had never felt more amazing or more afraid. It was almost too much pleasure.

He brought his mouth to hers and his tongue lashed her in time with his body, so that her soul had no chance to recover. She was trembling, digging her nails into his back and even then failing to stay on earth. She was floating high above it. Then she was flying, soaring to heaven, her body barely holding together as release from sexual tension radiated from her.

Her voice was a loud cry and her hands pummelled his back. She gripped onto him for dear life, but nothing could stop the wave. It carried her until she was limp and breathless, but the pleasure didn't stop. He moved harder, shifting her with him, moving his mouth to her breast, rolling her nipple in the warmth of his mouth, and she sobbed at how good it felt. Her nerves were already over-sensitised.

He drove into her harder now, and she knew a second wave was coming. She could feel it building, as loud as the thunder outside. She tilted her head back and he kissed her neck, grating his teeth over the exposed flesh. She caught his mouth, tasting him, kissing him with all her passion and all her truth. Kissing away the lies she'd told him, making sure he understood.

This—this was who she was. This was real.

She wrapped her legs around him and he thrust deeper. She cried out, and the second her world began to shake he chased after her, linking his fingers through hers and lifting them above her head as their bodies ascended to the heavens together.

It wasn't sex. It wasn't making love. It was something else entirely. An experience unique to the two of them and to that moment.

She held him inside her, her legs tight around his waist, her hands pinned by him, their bodies in utter unison. Complete agreement.

His chest was moving with the force of his breathing. He brought his head closer, pressing his forehead against hers.

'Worth the wait,' he said, and smiled, his eyes so full of feeling when they met hers that a new wave of guilt lashed her.

'The wait was pretty excruciating,' she whispered. 'For both of us.'

He shifted, and she felt him move inside her, sparking new recognition and desire.

She expelled a shaking breath. 'Yesterday...' she murmured, hiding her eyes from his.

He brought his mouth to hers and kissed the corner of her lips. 'Yes?'

'You...you said you didn't want me.'

He shook his head. 'I didn't want you like that. I didn't want to be just another man who'd taken advantage of you.'

Tilly crashed her eyes shut, still hiding herself from him. The lie of who she was had begun to eat at her gut, but he mistook her gesture as one of embarrassment.

'I don't care who you were with before me,' he said seriously. 'I hate the idea of you being out of control drunk and asking men to sleep with you. I hate the idea that a lot of men probably give in to you.' He stroked her cheek. 'But that's not me. It's not us. And what's happening between us is all that I'm interested in.'

Her heart turned over at the words that meant so much to her.

She resolutely ignored the other words—the suppositions that had no reference to *her*, Matilda Morgan. The assumptions that should be laid at Cressida's feet, but not at hers.

'You were angry outside.'

His laugh was a deep rumble. *'Si.'*

'Why?'

'Because, *carina maldestra*, I do not like seeing you hurt. Wet. Cold. Or in any danger. It is the first time I have looked at a woman and wanted to...'

'What?' she asked, pushing at his shoulder, needing to hear the conclusion of the sentence.

'Keep her from harm,' he admitted with a self-deprecating smile.

Her stomach squeezed. She tried not to read too much into the admission, but how could she not? She smiled up at him, and her voice was weakened by emotion when she said, 'You don't need to protect me.'

His laugh was rueful. 'No. I am starting to realise that *you* are not the one in danger here.'

CHAPTER NINE

'IT'S NOT CALMING DOWN,' she said, leaning forward, scanning the sky.

He stood behind her, his arms wrapped around her waist, bunching the sheet she'd donned toga-style at her middle.

'No.' He dropped his lips to her neck, kissing her softly.

She spun in the circle of his arms, her smile radiant. Her hair was wild around her face and her eyes were a glorious green. Her neck was pink from his stubble. He leaned down and kissed her mouth gently, smiling against her lips.

'I used to be terrified of storms,' she confided, dipping her fingers into the elasticised waist of his boxer shorts, revelling in the sensation of his smooth buttocks, almost unable to comprehend that she was free to touch him so intimately.

'They can be frightening.'

'Yes. Though I think I'll always have a special liking for them after this.' Her grin was shy. She reached up and cupped his cheeks, staring at him, trying to see if there was any regret in her heart or on his face.

There was none.

'I should go and check on the generator,' he said, with obvious reluctance.

'Really?'

He nodded, stepping away from her. 'Really. It should be on by now. There could be more of a problem than I anticipated.'

'But you'll get soaked again.'

'And I know just how to get warm and dry,' he pointed out, turning towards the front door.

Tilly watched him walk out with a sigh, but as he reached the door she called after him. 'Rio? Where are those plans? I might as well have a look at them.'

His face clouded with something she didn't comprehend, but his nod was curt.

'Of course.'

He moved back into the cabin, disappearing into his bedroom. Curious, she padded closer to the door and peered in. There was a desk against the wall, with a large drawer. He pulled out some old pages, and a yellowed piece of paper smaller than the rest which, she saw as he brought it closer, showed hand sketches. The others looked as if they'd been professionally put together.

His eyes held hers as he handed them over, his jaw set.

She didn't notice. 'Thanks.'

He spun and left the cabin while Tilly moved into the kitchen. A cursory inspection showed the bench was clean, with the exception of a couple of crumbs from the toast he'd presumably made that morning. She wiped it with a cloth anyway, and then placed the drawings down.

It took her several minutes to comprehend what

had been drawn, to orientate herself to the angle of the plans and imagine the buildings that the architect had envisaged.

They were brilliant.

Instead of a large-scale hotel, several cabins had been drawn—some with one bedroom, others with several, allowing for families or groups. The architect had marked an area of the beach to be roped off for activities. On the other side of the island the architect had sketched in a ten-storey building with a pool that ran right to the sand of the beach. And there was the cable car over the volcano, with a restaurant perched right on top, so diners could peek in as they ate.

The door slamming heralded Rio's return.

'These are incredible,' she called, flicking to the next one, which showed the elevations for the buildings.

He made a grunt of agreement and she turned to face him.

'You're wet,' she said, the words breathy.

'Yes.' His eyes glittered when they met hers. He lifted a finger and pulled it through the air, beckoning her towards him.

She didn't hesitate.

He pushed at the sheet, discarding it easily, and lifted her to sit on the edge of the kitchen bench. Her legs were naked and he moved between them, moving his mouth over hers. She pushed at his jeans, loosening them, and he stepped out of them. Naked and so close to her. She edged forward, wanting him again already, *needing* him.

His hands pulled at her legs and she lay back on the bench, her voice a hoarse cry as he took possession of her, running his hands down her front, teasing her skin, delighting her breasts.

He took her as though his life—and hers—depended on it. He gripped her hips, holding her as he pushed deep into her core, and then his hand moved to the entrance of her womanhood. His fingers brushed against her as he moved and her body shook and trembled with the potency of need.

She exploded just as the lights flicked back to life and everything was bright again. She wrapped her legs around him and he came with her, chasing her, whispering to her in his own tongue, imprinting himself on her for evermore.

She lay there, staring at the ceiling, her mind slow, her eyes heavy with spent desire, her pulse racing. She stared and waited for her breathing to return to normal.

He pressed a finger against her lips and she looked up at him, a smile on her face. 'The power's back.'

He nodded. 'Apparently.'

She pushed herself up to sit, but didn't relinquish the grip her legs had around his waist. She curled her arms around his neck, tangling her fingers into the hair at his nape. His lips sought hers and they were gentle, sweet, curious.

She breathed in deeply, smelling him, tasting him. Loving him.

'These plans are amazing.' She pulled away just enough to see his face. 'Have you looked at them properly?'

Again his jaw clenched, and this time she did notice.

It wasn't until an hour later, after they'd showered

and changed into dry clothes, that she began to suspect why.

'Rio?' she called, her head bent over the yellow
page with the sketches. 'This is a house,' she murmured. 'Not a hotel.'

He was reading the book she'd bought him, and the
sight did all sorts of funny things to her equilibrium.

'Yes. It was an option that was being considered,
apparently.'

'A beautiful house,' she said wistfully, turning it
over to view the floor plan that was on the back.
'Though quite the change from this little cabin,' she
quipped, for the house was three storeys with tremen-
dous glass windows overlooking the ocean.

He was watching her, as if he sensed that she
was about to discover something. Something he had
guarded carefully all his life.

'Rio?' She frowned as her eye caught the corner of
the plan. 'What was your mother's name?'

He was quiet, so she lifted her gaze to him. 'It was
Rosa, wasn't it?'

She looked at another page and saw the same name
printed neatly in the corner.

Rosa Mastrangelo

'Your mother did these plans.' She moved away
from the bench and crossed to him, sitting on his lap
so that she could wrap an arm around his neck and
hold him. Instinctively she knew that this changed
things. That she'd found something that would be
hard for him to talk about.

'And you were left this island.' She stroked his cheek, lost in thought. 'By your father...'

His expression gave little away; it made it impossible for her to forget that this was who he was, first and foremost. A successful tycoon who could control his emotions easily—who'd made a fortune in his ability to do just that.

'Am I right?'

Only the pulsing in the thick column of his neck as he swallowed showed that her supposition was correct.

'A month ago,' he said, by way of confirmation.

His expression was a firm mask, emotionless and resonating with strength. But she knew him too well to buy it. He was hurting. This strong, powerful man was in pain and she wanted to fix it.

She shifted, straddling him so that she could stare straight into his eyes. 'Tell me.'

His face shifted. A small shake of his head, a twist of his mouth. 'There is not much to tell. As a rule, *cara*, I do not speak of him. Ever.'

'I feel like you and I are people who would break rules together,' she said with a small smile. 'Who was he?'

His expression was contained. Still, she understood his struggle.

'You don't trust me?' she prompted quietly, padding her thumb over his cheek.

'The strange thing is that I do.' His lips quirked into a downward twist as he studied her thoughtfully. 'For the first time in my life I *want* to confide in someone about this.'

Warmth spread through her. She waited, enjoying her closeness to him as he searched for words.

'My father was Piero Varelli.' He looked at her, waiting for comprehension to dawn.

He saw the moment recognition lit her eyes. 'The shipping guy?'

'Ships.' He jerked his head in a small nod. 'Planes. *Si.*'

Outrage fizzed in her gut. 'You're saying your father was a *multi-millionaire*...'

'A billionaire,' he corrected.

'And he let you and your mother...?'

His smile was without humour. 'You see, perhaps, why I do not have time for him.'

'Oh, yes,' she agreed with true anger. 'But I don't understand. How could he refuse to help you?'

He expelled a harsh sigh. 'He was married when he met my mother.' The words rang with bitterness. 'He tricked her into loving him because it suited him— or perhaps he thought he loved her. But he didn't. Not enough to tell her the truth—to tell her he was married.'

With an enormous effort she kept her own guilt far from her mind. There would be a time to reckon with her choices and the consequences of them. She didn't want to face it yet. But already remorse was washing over her, no matter how she tried to keep it at bay. She was lying to him. She was lying to him just as his father had lied to his mother.

Only this was different. Wasn't it?

'And she didn't know?'

'She was young and in love. My father was rich and charismatic. She'd never known anyone like him.

It was not difficult for her to lose her heart.' His eyes met hers. 'Right here, on this island. She spent some time here with him, touring it just as you have been.'

The notion of history repeating itself filled her with a strange sense of wariness.

'And she got pregnant?'

'Right. And that's when he offered to pay for an abortion.' His face shimmered with determination.

'Your mother must have been so upset.'

'I'm sure she was. But she focussed on making a life for us.'

'I don't understand why he didn't pay child support. And I don't understand why your mother let him get away with that,' she said quietly.

His eyes were hard in his handsome face. 'I think she knew she could have. But she was proud. *So* proud. He made it obvious he didn't want her—or me—and she was not going to beg.'

'I'm sorry, Rio.'

He brushed away the apology, shifting a little and reminding Tilly of their powerful attraction.

'He got in contact with me about five years ago, trying to "connect", as he called it.'

Indignation rushed through her. 'How dare he?' she said fiercely. 'After all that time! And what you'd been through! What did you tell him?'

His laugh was short. 'Exactly that. His explanation helped me understand, I suppose, though ultimately it just proved how selfish he was.'

'What did he say? How did he explain it?'

His eyes clouded and he shook his head.

She dipped her head forward and kissed him, letting her mouth tell him what was in her heart and soul.

'What did he say?' she murmured, keeping her face close to his.

'That he was married. And, yes, he loved his wife—very much, he said.' Rio's scathing tone showed how little he believed that. 'Carina—that's her name—and he were high school sweethearts. They had been trying to conceive a child for ten years. He told me that it took its toll on their marriage. That he met my mother and was captivated by her.'

Tilly was quiet, but inside she was raging against this selfish man who'd conned Rio's mother into an affair. 'And she didn't know he was married,' Tilly clarified.

'No. Not until she told him about me. That's when he told her that he and Carina had been trying for a baby. News of my mother's pregnancy would have been devastating for her.' His smile was flat. 'My mother actually felt sorry for Carina. Can you believe it?'

'Yes,' Tilly said honestly. 'I can tell what kind of woman your mother was, and I imagine her heart would have been easily touched.'

His eyes flashed with unknown emotion as they met Tilly's. 'He told my mother that he would never acknowledge me. That he would never speak to her again. So *she* was left devastated instead of his wife,' he said softly.

'How awful.' She frowned. 'You said he contacted you a few years ago?'

He made a noise of agreement. 'Eventually they adopted. A boy. Then, six years ago, their son died. And a year after that he left Carina. Or she left him. I do not know. Only that he suddenly felt a compulsion to meet with me, his biological son.' His expression was harsh.

Tears, unwanted and hot, stung Tilly's eyes. 'You must have been—'

'Furious?' he interrupted. 'I was. But by then I had established myself. I had a fortune behind me, and I had learned to live without my mother. And, obviously, my father. What did I need from him? A man who had given my mother only heartache?'

His bitterness touched Tilly deep in her heart. She understood it, and yet it was impossible not to grieve for both Rio *and* Piero.

'I could not look at him without seeing my mother's pain. The way she'd been when she was ill. Weakened by cancer and chemotherapy, pale and hollowed out, as if all the living had been scooped from inside her. I wanted nothing to do with him. *Nothing.* And I told him so. I particularly did not want him to have the satisfaction of claiming me as his prodigal son.'

His eyes were loaded with enmity.

'How did their son die?' she murmured softly.

'An accident. Drink-driving.'

'He was hit?'

'He was the drunk. He collided with a tree. Thankfully it was only him who died.'

How awful for Rio—to have discovered his father and also a brother he might have known and loved if only things had been different.

'When you met with your father, did you feel anything?'

'No.'

'Nothing?'

'*Niente.*'

'And yet,' she said softly, cautiously, 'she loved him. And he is in you.'

She tapped a finger against his heart, her lips pressing against his gently.

His rebuke was swift and determined. 'I am who I am because of my mother. Not him.'

She ran her fingers over his cheek. 'And he died a month ago?' she murmured.

At this, Rio's face briefly flashed with an emotion she didn't comprehend. Regret? Sorrow?

'And he left me Prim'amore.'

She expelled a soft breath. 'I suppose he felt it was the least he could do.'

'I don't know. I think he was a stubborn, selfish man who wanted to make sure I faced this.' His eyes glittered. 'Because it suited him that I should.'

Tilly stroked his cheek. 'His wife must have been devastated when he died and she found out about you.'

'She still doesn't know,' he said, with a flicker of something in his eyes.

'But…he left you Prim'amore.'

'And a lot of money I will never touch.' It was a dark admission.

'But surely when she saw his will…?'

'They were divorced,' he reminded her gently. 'She did not go to his funeral.'

'Did you?'

Something like disappointment marked his face. '*Si.*' And then, as though he needed to defend the action, he said angrily, 'I know my mother would have wished it. It felt like I was closing the chapter on them.'

Her heart squeezed with anguish. 'I'm so sorry for you, Rio.'

'I do not want the link between that bastard and me to become known. Not now. Nothing would be served by it being made public. I certainly see no benefit in hurting Carina's feelings.'

'That's why you're hurrying to sell the island. Why you're handling it yourself,' she said, remembering the way his face had been so adamant when she'd first stepped off the boat. *'No agents,'* he'd said, as though the very idea was anathema to him.

'You know what the press is like.' His eyes met hers, grey to green. 'You, of all people, understand about their intrusion into things that do not concern them. I want a quick, private sale. Only three people in the world know about this—you, me and your father.'

And Cressida, Tilly thought with a sudden warning feeling of panic. And whoever *she* had mentioned it to in passing. Adrenalin spiked inside her. The real heiress was hardly discreet, and she would have no reason to suspect that Rio needed his link to Prim'amore kept secret.

'I've been here a month,' he said, the words darkened by memories. 'I came to the island after my father died, intending only to stay a day or two.'

'And yet you've been here a month?' she asked with interest.

Because he felt close to his mother here. Because he was saying goodbye—to his father, yes, but to the father he might have had, should have had. He was making his peace with a bitter resentment that would eat him alive if he let it.

He shrugged his broad shoulders, tilting his head back to see her more clearly. 'I want to sell this island and as quickly as possible. Having anything from him feels like a betrayal.'

Tilly nodded, but inside she wasn't sure she agreed with him. 'This island is…' She bit down on her lip, trying to find words for the strange idea that was forming inside her. 'It's like it's a *part* of you,' she said, with the tilt of her head that Rio had learned indicated she was deep in thought. 'They fell in love here; you were conceived here.'

His grunt showed how little he thought that mattered. 'This island is too little, too late. It is a reminder of what a weak, pathetic man my father really was.' His brows drew together. 'And yet my mother loved him. She loved him all her life. Even at the end he was all she talked of when she faded in and out of consciousness.'

Sadness swamped them.

When Rio spoke next, it was as if from a long way away. 'When my mother used to tell me about him, about how they'd met, it was like she'd been hit by a truck. *Gravità*, she called it. Gravity. Like he was earth and she was floating in the heavens and *bam!* She met him and fell…crashed. Burned, as it happened.'

His smile was tight, and it gave way to a rueful grimace.

'I never understood that. How could she meet a married man and fall in love with him? How could she ignore common sense?'

'She didn't know about Carina,' Tilly answered softly. 'So far as she believed she'd simply fallen in love with a man.'

'How could she love a lie? That's what it was. It was all fake.'

Tilly swallowed, but panic made her blood flash hot and cold. 'Not to her.'

'No, not to her. But the whole idea of that kind of feeling is foreign to me.' He shifted, his fingers tangling in the hem of her dress, pushing it so that he could connect with her bare thighs. 'It *was*, anyway.'

'Oh?' *Bang, bang, bang*—her heart slammed hard against her ribcage.

'Mmm…' His hands pushed higher, gripping her legs right at the top, his fingers stroking the sensitive flesh of her inner thighs. 'Until I met you I thought love at first sight was a lie invented by Hollywood.'

Her breath caught in her throat as her entire world shifted into blinding focus. Had he just said he loved her? That he was falling in love with her? Hadn't she been feeling that since she'd first met him? Or had she misunderstood?

Doubt was quick to follow hope, but love was unmistakable and ever-present.

'Cara…' He spoke with gravelled determination. 'When I decide I want something, I go after it. Do you know how long it took me to realise I wanted you?'

She shook her head, not trusting her voice to speak.

'Minutes. When you fell into the ocean and laughed about it. You were beautiful. The most beautiful woman I'd ever seen. But it was more than that. You were humble.'

Happiness and her future hovered in front of her, like a butterfly with mesmerising wings. But no vision could wipe out the awful truth.

She'd fallen in love with him, too. But she'd lied to him. And once he knew would he forgive her?

She already knew the answer to that. She'd heard the way he'd spoken of Marina, his ex. But she'd lied about being pregnant with his baby—surely a greater betrayal than this?

A throb of resentment shifted inside her. She wanted to be honest with him, but what then? Could she tell him and be sure Cressida would never find out? And what if Cressida learned the truth? Tilly had already given the money to her brother; the lie was bought and paid for.

'The first time I have ever told a woman I love her and I get silence.'

She laughed, a husky sound, as the present sucked her back towards perfection. 'I didn't expect it.'

'Nor did I. Nothing about this is expected.'

'Look. It's clearing.'

Tilly yawned, her head pressed against his shoulder. He stroked her hair absentmindedly, his gaze settled on the wall opposite. It was not late, but a day in the darkened cabin, distracted by so much emotion, had left Tilly tired. The storm was finally abating, though, and a hint of sunshine crested through the window.

He shifted abruptly, placing her head against a pillow. 'Stay here.'

It was a command she didn't care to disobey. Her body was languid and floppy after being pleasured by him again and again. Her heart was full to overflowing with his suggestion of love.

She let her eyes drift closed, but didn't sleep. How

could she? There was a constant shuffling of things, and the regular slamming of the door to keep her awake.

She listened, though, with a smile playing about her lips. A smile that was wilfully ignoring the prickly path that lay before her.

She wasn't who he thought she was. And if she revealed the truth to him how would he react?

Her heart turned over, and briefly a frown crossed her features. Imagining life outside the island had become impossible. She had joked, on her first day on Prim'amore, that it was as though they were the only two people on earth. Yet that was how she felt after a few days alone with Rio.

The pressures that had brought this to be—worries about her brother, compassion for Cressida—all came to nought when she was with Rio. Could they not just remain on the island for ever? Pretending the outside world did not exist? With a few trips to Capri to secure essentials?

Life would go on; the world would spin. And she would spin with Rio.

Her heart.

Her soul.

Her other.

'I'm ready.'

She blinked, opened her eyes, yawning as she focussed on him.

'For what?'

'Come.'

She followed him towards the door of the cabin and down the steps. The sand was cold and wet beneath her bare feet, but she didn't care. She wanted to look up at him, but a glow in the distance called to her.

Several candles were set out in the sand, and in the middle a makeshift bed.

'You did this?'

He linked his fingers through hers and lifted her hand to his lips, then pulled her towards the blanket.

They walked slowly, breathing in the scent of fresh air in the wake of the passing storm. It was on the horizon now—a dark cloud dissipating into the sea.

'You *must* have mixed feelings about selling the island?'

He squeezed her fingers, perhaps to acknowledge that he'd heard the question, and then focussed his gaze out to sea. 'No.'

'Even though it's where they fell in love?' she murmured, saddened to imagine him selling it and that link being lost for ever.

'Their love broke her.'

'*Cancer* broke her,' she corrected pragmatically, wrapping an arm around his waist as they walked.

'I know that.' He expelled an angry breath, then cleared his throat. 'When she was dying, at the end, she spoke of him almost more than she spoke to me. He was so heavy in her mind and heart. I couldn't ever forgive him for that.'

His smile was tight.

'He cheated on his wife. Mistake number one. Never cheat; never lie. He left my mother pregnant and alone, and never once checked to see that we were comfortable. And we weren't.'

He cleared his throat again. They were almost at the blanket and he slowed a little.

'I was twenty when I made my first million. If she'd managed to live a few more years I could have given her comfort and security…'

Tilly's stomach churned. 'I think… I think she wanted you to be happy and smart and brave, and you are. I think you were the greatest gift in her life.'

His smile was perfunctory. He nodded towards the carpet and she moved to sit on it, but her eyes stayed glued to his face.

'I really am sorry for what you've gone through.'

He shrugged. 'I do not think your childhood has been a walk in the park either,' he said pragmatically.

She thought of Cressida, and then she thought of Art, and it confused her. Art adored Cressida. Tilly knew he did. But he didn't understand her. And Cressida was not the kind of daughter the businessman knew how to work with. She was beautiful, and she was smart, but she was smart with people and things—not numbers and contracts.

Cressida Wyndham was never going to step into Art's shoes and start running the family business. She didn't want to. She wanted to live her own life and to live a darned good life, too, with all the luxuries that most people could only dream of.

But that wasn't exactly Cressida's fault. She was a product of her upbringing.

Speaking to Rio, and reflecting on Cressida, could only make Tilly recognise her luck in having been born into the Morgan family. Sure, Jack was a bit anxiety-inducing—especially with his recent interest in gambling—but essentially things for the Morgans were simple. They loved each other and they were there for each other.

That was family for Tilly.

'I don't think I have any right to complain,' she said softly, settling herself onto the rug and staring out at the ocean.

It was angry and churning, and the sun was a fluorescent orange as it tunnelled through the woolly clouds.

'Why not?'

Tilly put herself in Cressida's shoes, but they were pinching now—leaving blisters she knew she didn't want to deal with.

'Because I had everything growing up.' She smiled at him as he sat beside her, glad when he put an arm around her shoulders and pulled her close. 'My family life is idyllic compared to yours,' she said seriously. 'No offence.'

He stroked her hair. 'None taken.'

She turned to face him, feeling safe and complete in the circle of his arms. 'Why did you do this?'

His eyes linked to hers before flicking back to the storm-ravaged ocean. 'I have never known a woman like you before.'

She saved that little admission for revelling in later.

'Most of the women I have slept with have been good for only one purpose.'

Jealousy was a fever inside her. 'I see,' she responded crisply.

'I have not wanted to know what moved their hearts and minds.' He ran his fingers over her shoulder, sending goosebumps of fire and ice through her soul. 'With you, I want to know everything and I want to see everything. The sun setting after a storm like this? I want to share it with *you* and only you. I want to feel your thoughts as we watch it together. *Cara*, I do not know I could ever watch a sunset without knowing you would see it with me.'

CHAPTER TEN

THE SOUND OF a motor broke through their solitude. Tilly spun in the water, her eyes scanning the horizon, a frown nudging across her face when she saw a boat coming close to shore. It took her a moment to recognise it as the speedboat that had first brought her to the island, almost a week earlier.

'Rafaelo,' Rio murmured beside her, standing in the water and striding towards the shore.

He was more beautiful than any person had a right to be. Broad-shouldered, strong, tanned. She stared after him as he emerged from the crystalline ocean, droplets running down his back, and her stomach swooned, as if she was on a rollercoaster that had gained speed and was heading into its deep descent.

She watched as Rio moved to the boat and stood, one hand on his hip, his chest shamelessly ridged, his expression relaxed as he spoke to the old man. He threw his head back and laughed, then pointed towards Tilly and laughed again.

They were too far away for her to hear what they were discussing, but when Rafaelo pointed at the generator she got the gist.

The engine revved again and then Rafaelo was

leaving, waving at Tilly as he passed, and Rio was returning to Tilly, cutting easily through the water with his strong legs.

Her heart flipped.

She didn't want to leave him.

Ever.

Yet that was an inevitability.

Unless…

Unconsciously, she frowned as possibilities and thoughts ran through her mind. Unless she could find a way to tell him the truth. She would need to speak to Cressida first—to promise Cressida it wouldn't go any further. And then she'd need to be sure Rio would understand why she'd gone along with the charade. She'd need him to know she hadn't ever intended to deceive him.

'Rafaelo wanted to see how the island had fared in the storm.' Rio wrapped his arms around Tilly under the water and she curled her legs around his midsection, enjoying the feeling of being close to him underwater. 'He's going to pick up some supplies from Capri and drop back later today.'

She made a sound of agreement, but it rankled.

His laugh showed that he understood. 'You are pouting.'

Tilly made an effort to straighten her expression. 'I am not.'

'He won't stay long,' Rio promised, kissing the side of her mouth.

Was she *that* transparent?

'Does he live on Capri?' she asked, purely to move conversation away from how selfishly she was guarding her time with Rio.

'Yes. He's looked after the island for a long time.'

'Did he know your dad?'

He dipped his head forward. 'And my mother, it turns out,' Rio murmured.

'Really?'

'He is the same age as her. When my mother came to stay on the island he came and laid down a lot of the tracks, helped her find the volcano. He comes and tinkers every month or so—it's been a long time since my father came to the island and the cabin needs attention. The generator… The bike…'

'How does he feel about you selling it?'

His laugh was unexpected.

She angled her face towards his. 'What? Why is that funny?'

'It just hadn't occurred to me to ask him for his emotional assessment of my real estate choices.'

She felt heat darken her cheeks. 'You don't think it's reasonable?'

'You think if he is upset I should keep it?'

She turned to face the island. The white sand, the green trees, the blue sky behind it and the cabin that had been the place of *her* Prim'amore.

'I think your father would feel pretty aggrieved if I backed out now,' he said. 'Making his daughter my lover and then reneging on a deal that is almost locked in.'

A shiver danced along her spine. There was something in the way he spoke that said so much more than the words alone. It created the impression of a future. A future with Art, Tilly and Rio. A future that was impossible to envisage. No, that wasn't true. She could see it—she just couldn't imagine reaching out and grasping it. It was like trying to catch rain in your hands.

This wouldn't work. It could never be more than this week. Unless she could somehow work something out with Cressida. And even then…? What if Rio didn't forgive her?

'You didn't *make* me your lover,' she pointed out, surprised at how normal her voice sounded when her heart was shattering just a little. 'It was definitely mutual.'

She was distracted, so when he kissed her it felt like their first kiss—except so much better. Because he loved her, and she loved him, and their kiss was full of that.

'I am addicted to you,' he growled against her neck, flicking his tongue against the sensitive skin that covered her racing pulse.

'That's mutual, too.'

The ocean was lapping quietly, the sun was warm overhead, the air smelt like salt and Rio was beside her—still working, but beside her. And she needed him there.

Tilly's eyes were heavy—and no wonder. Sleep had been snatched between making love to Rio—and they'd done that a lot. Her body was sore all over, but deliciously so. Every movement reminded her of how he'd claimed her, of how she had moved over him, taking him deep inside her. She stretched a little, sighing and letting her eyes drift shut as sleep began to press down on her.

Rio's hand on her hair was perfect. Gentle, reassuring. Loving.

Her smile widened. She felt like the cat who'd got the cream. Future be damned; in this perfect moment she was going to enjoy it.

She was almost asleep when the purring of a boat's engine penetrated her haze of pleasure.

'Rafaelo…' he murmured.

She pushed up onto her elbows in time to see the older man push an anchor overboard.

'Stay here,' Rio said, and the words were a command she found incredibly sexy, even when a part of her knew she should be offended at being ordered around.

She opened her mouth to say something, but he brought his body over hers and she was reminded of how much she wanted him—needed him—and how incredible he felt on top of her. Her throat was parched, her mind blank.

'You look too perfect. I want to see you like this always.' He kissed her quickly, and then stood with an athleticism she couldn't help but admire.

'We're going to go and check for damage. Shouldn't be more than an hour.'

'An hour?' She pouted again and he laughed.

'Half an hour,' he amended, winking and then turning towards the ocean and jogging the rest of the way to the boat.

She watched, not bothering to hide her interest, as he took a cardboard box from the boat and began to walk towards the cabin.

She stood reluctantly, tiredness still fogging her, but a plan giving urgency to her movements.

'Mind if I check my email?' she called towards

him, striding away on a trajectory that would lead her to the cabin too.

They arrived at the deck together.

'No. I will dial it in for you now.'

'I can manage,' she said, and he arched a brow.

'Without electrocuting yourself?'

'Hey!' She punched his arm playfully.

He grinned, pulling the door open and holding it with his foot so she could precede him into the house.

'What's in the box?' she asked, peeking over the top as he walked behind her.

'Groceries. Batteries. Candles. And newspapers.'

'Ready for a siege?'

'Or another blackout,' he pointed out.

He placed the box on the kitchen bench, then moved to his laptop. He opened it up and logged into the phone's signal, then straightened.

She looked so beautiful—so different from the images he'd seen of her in the press. In those pictures she was always made up to within an inch of her life, her body bared for the world to see. Here, she was stunning, but in a completely natural way, her hair shimmering, her eyes enormous, her skin fresh.

He kissed the tip of her nose. 'I won't be long.'

She watched him walk towards the door.

When he reached it, he turned to face her. *'Cara?'*

She waited, her breath held, for him to speak.

'Don't go tomorrow.'

Another command. One her heart and soul wanted her to obey.

'I'm sorry?' she whispered, not sure if it was an apology or a question.

'Don't go. Not yet.'

She bit down on her lower lip and tears built at the back of her eyes, threatening to spill down her cheeks.

'Rafaelo's waiting,' she said in response, the words moist.

He nodded—a curt tilt of his head. '*Si, lo so.* And yet we need to discuss this.'

'We will. But not now.'

Not until she'd emailed Cressida.

He seemed to take that as acquiescence. The smile he flashed her as he walked out through the door was filled with a confidence that bordered on arrogance.

And it made her heart swell even more.

She made herself a coffee—or a kip in a cup, as she liked to think of it—and then moved to his laptop. Even that made her smile, at how much it reminded her of him. She ran her fingertips over the case of the screen, her pulse tingling. She sipped her coffee and loaded up a browser.

Her inbox was full—little one-liners from her mother, a chatty email from Jack that filled her with hope that he was sounding more like himself again, and a few from Art, asking where to locate various files or emails.

She dealt with the business ones first, apologising for having been out of contact, then she opened up her Facebook profile. It was a time-waster she couldn't afford. She'd peruse her friends' holiday photos and new baby pictures another time. When she was back in England. When this was over and reality was intruding.

She clicked on to Cressida's profile, marvelling as always at how similar-looking they were, and opened up a new message to her.

Hey, I hope you're having a good time. Something's happened here and…

And what? *I can't keep your secret? The secret you paid me thirty thousand pounds for?* She groaned and deleted the sentence, staring at the blinking cursor.

She wasn't afraid of Cressida. Not at all. But Matilda Morgan was honourable and loyal, and she'd promised Cressida that she would do this.

Was it Cressida's fault that Matilda had fallen head over heels in love with Rio Mastrangelo?

Hi, Cressida. It's Tilly.

Crap. That was even worse. She'd know who was messaging her! Matilda deleted it, then took a big gulp of coffee.

Cressida, we need to speak.

She loitered over the 'send' button for a moment and then hit it before she could second-guess what she was doing. She bit down on her lip, and had gone back to her emails when a 'ping' noise indicated that she'd received a new message.

Her breath held, she clicked back into Facebook and saw a little green circle beside Cressida's name. She opened the message up, her nerves firing in every direction as Cressida began to type. The little dots moved frantically and Tilly waited with impatient panic.

Finally words appeared, and Tilly leaned close to the screen as she read them.

Hey, babes! What's up? Hope you're having a bloody
ball. I know I am. You are such a superstar for doing
this for me! I owe you. xxxxxxxx

Tilly couldn't help the smile that pulled at her lips.
Cressida was extravagant with praise and censure.
She was one hundred and ten per cent sure of how
she felt at all times.

Tilly ran her fingertip over the space bar as she
tried to find words. Eventually she typed her reply,
testing the water with a small white lie.

Don't thank me yet. I think Rio suspects something.

The response was immediate.

You're not serious?

Tilly expelled a breath and began to type again.

Yes. Did you know he was going to be the one showing me around? For a whole week?

There was a pause and Tilly suspected Cressida
was doing her own word-searching, looking for a
way to explain why she hadn't been upfront about
that.

Now that you mention it, I think Daddy did say that
might be the case. Something about not wanting
people to know he was selling the island.

Tilly ground her teeth together.

A heads-up would have been nice. We're sharing a tiny cabin…

Cressida sent a little laughing face emoji which made Tilly roll her eyes.

It's not funny.

Tilly's response was another emoji and then:

LOL! Sorry. Just imagining Miss Prim & Proper spending a week on a gorgeous island with that spectacular piece of man. What a wasted opportunity. Maybe I should have gone instead…

Tilly expelled an angry breath.

Actually… she began to write, thinking through a way to tell Cressida the truth that wouldn't result in gossip spreading like wildfire.

'Urghhhh!' she shouted into the cabin.

It was useless. She was caught between a rock and a hard place. If she told Cressida that she'd fallen in love with Rio, Cressida might tell the world—and Tilly didn't want that.

Although… Realisation fired inside her. Cressida was as bound by silence as Tilly was. How could Cressida spread the news about Tilly and Rio without owning up to her own part in the scheme, thereby admitting to her deception?

The thing is, I like him.

Tilly sent the message, instinctively disliking the lukewarm sentiment.

And I want to see him again.

There was a pause. A long silence.

No.

Tilly read the single-word response with indignation.

What do you mean, 'no'?

The dots began to move and Tilly waited, gnawing on her lower lip and fidgeting with her fingers in her lap.

Part of our deal is that you don't tell anyone. That's what I pay you for. What good is it having a doppelgänger if I can't trust you?

Tilly squeezed her eyes shut. Thirty thousand pounds. The money she'd given Jack to save his life. Or at least his kneecaps.

Can we find a way around this? Tilly responded, her heart pounding, her eyes wet.

What do you suggest? If you tell him, he'll tell Dad. And that's not our deal.

Tilly swiped at her eyes, pushing the tears away.

I'm going to see him again.

Silence.
Tilly stared at the computer, but no dots were moving.
Finally, Cressida began to type.

If you tell Rio, I'll tell Dad. And not just about this. About all the jobs you've done for me. I'm sure he'd be fascinated to hear how his golden-girl PA has been lying to him for years.

Tilly's cheeks flushed pink.

Come on, Cressida. I'm not trying to ruin anything for you—I think Rio would keep this to himself.

Tilly waited, her body radiating with silent tension.

It's your decision. Don't forget to send my 30k back if you tell him, though.

The words were black and white, and Tilly saw them through a veil of stars.
A memory of Jack's face, so grateful, so relieved when she'd given him the cheque, flashed before her.
What a mess.

I have to go. Just remember, Tilly, you've got as much to lose in this as I do.

Cressida's little green dot disappeared, signalling that she'd logged off. Tilly still stared at the screen, though, re-reading their conversation with a falling feeling.

She had to tell Rio.

Surely she could get a bank loan for that amount, and repay Cressida? Still, loyalty strained at her heart. It was hardly Cressida's fault that Tilly had fallen in love with Rio. Cressida had every right to expect Tilly to uphold their agreement. Sure, she'd reacted like a cornered cat, but Tilly could hardly blame her.

With a grunt of annoyance she clicked out of Facebook, and out of her emails, and shut the lid on the laptop. Her coffee cup was empty but she was still tired.

Not from sleep-deprivation now so much as mental exhaustion. She'd turned the problem over again and again and there was still no answer. Nothing.

Except that she had to tell Rio. Somehow she had to make him understand that it had been innocent. She hadn't set out to deceive him, and she didn't want to deceive him for a moment longer.

He was gone longer than the appointed half-hour, though. An hour went by, then another thirty minutes, and she was contemplating going to look for him when he appeared at the doorway. He was covered in sweat and dirt and she'd never wanted him more.

'Hi.'

Sadness bubbled through her. Despair, too. But nothing mattered more than being honest with him.

'Hi,' he responded.

'Everything okay?' she asked warily.

'A few fallen trees, rocks—nothing major. The path is blocked halfway up, so no more volcano visits for you.' His eyes narrowed. 'You look pale.'

'I'm just tired,' she lied, forcing an over-bright smile to her face.

He studied her thoughtfully and then shrugged, as though her answer satisfied him. After all, they hadn't got a lot of sleep the night before.

'I'm starving. I could eat a horse.' He pulled the fridge door open and peered inside.

Tilly moved behind him. 'Rio?'

He lifted out the platter they'd picked at the night before, still full of olives, cheese, grapes and *grissini*.

'Si, cara?'

'I need to talk to you about something.'

He placed the platter between them, peeling off the plastic wrap, his eyes probing hers. 'Go on.'

'I…'

I'm not who you think. I've been lying to you. I'm not Cressida Wyndham. You know nothing about me.

She groaned inwardly, her mouth unable to form the words she needed to say.

'I have to go back as planned.' She cleared her throat, and spun away from him, so that he wouldn't detect the grief in her features.

She stared out of the large window, but her eyes saw nothing. Nothing. A bleakness, an emptiness, was settling in around her.

His arms around her waist were delirium and despair.

'Then I will come with you,' he said, the words husky.

It was a promise that she wrapped in her hands and held close to her heart for a moment.

But only a moment, because reality made that impossible. How could she risk seeing him again? It

wouldn't take long, back in London, for him to realise that she was not Cressida, and then the secret
would be out anyway.

Her smile was weak.

He spun her in his arms and kissed her, first on
her mouth and then on her temples. He kissed her as
though he understood that she was broken in that moment, as though he wanted to glue her back together.

'Ti amo,' he said gently, lifting her up and cradling
her against his chest, carrying her until they reached
his bed, where he laid her down with the same rev-
erence with which he'd kissed her.

His mouth took hers and his hands reached under
her dress. His fingers hooked into the waistband of
her underwear and slowly he glided them down her
legs, his palms teasing her flesh as he removed the
scrap of fabric and dropped them to the floor.

'Whatever it is that worries you, I will fix it.' He
crouched at her feet and kissed her ankle, rolling his
tongue over the round bone before dragging it higher,
flicking just behind her knee, and higher still to the
sensitive flesh of her inner thighs.

She groaned when his tongue connected with her
womanhood, teasing her and driving all thought from
her mind. His fingers dug into her thighs as he parted
her legs, giving him access to her core.

She trembled.

The power of emotion and need he stirred washed
over her and she was both powerless and empow-
ered. It was an ancient act—one that they had made
uniquely their own. She tilted her hips and he kissed
higher, trailing a line to her belly button, his fingers

wrapping into the fabric of her dress, pushing it up with him.

He was gone then, and she groaned, her body unable to exist without his nearness, his touch, his attention. He pushed out of his shorts, and then he was back. She almost cried with relief. His mouth sought her once more, his tongue whispering against her folds. She felt her blood pressure was about to burst.

'Rio!' she cried out, rocking on the bed as orgasm broke around her. She tangled her hands in his hair, pulling at it, fire and flame ravaging her. A sheen of sweat glossed her pale flesh.

'I *never* want to stop this,' she murmured, not even aware of what she was saying.

'We won't,' he agreed, and his hands were parting her legs so that he could enter her, take her, make her his.

And she *was* his. Completely.

From the second he thrust into her she knew she would find a way to solve this—without hurting Cressida, without betraying her promises, and without losing Rio. There was some kind of magic out there *somewhere*. She just had to uncover it.

His hands were roughened by demand as they moved over her body, pushing at the dress until they found her breasts and cupped them. He groaned as he massaged their weight, his fingers teasing her sensitive nerves while he drove into her.

She was lost at sea. She arched her back and lifted her legs, and he dropped a hand, catching her thigh and holding it, holding her leg where it was, high in the air. He nipped at her calf with his teeth and she groaned.

It was sensual torment. She was a willing prisoner and would be for ever.

Pressure built; it was a dam about to burst. She could not contain it. She didn't want to. She caught hold of his shoulders as it broke and he was on top of the water, riding the wave with her, his body moving in unison with hers, pleasure dousing them together.

Their panting filled the room, and finally pleasure. Release. Relief.

She wrapped her arms around him and brushed her cheek to his.

She belonged here. With Rio.

Tilly couldn't have said how much time passed. Knew only that they lay together, bodies entwined, sweat mingling, needs satiated—for the moment—until he spoke.

'I was gone too long,' he said with a rueful grin. 'I was ready to punch Rafaelo when he suggested we tour yet another path.'

Her smile was wide on her face, her lips pink, her cheeks stained from desire. 'You're forgiven.'

He laughed. 'I'm glad.' He pressed a kiss against her forehead. 'Want to come and see the caves?'

'Caves?' she murmured, her eyes showing confusion.

'I said we'd get back to them, remember?'

She did—of course. She just hadn't thought of them since. She nodded. She would find a way to tell him the truth, and in the meantime what harm could come from enjoying every minute they had left on the island?

'Sounds perfect.'

And it was.

The caves were every bit as beautiful as she'd imagined. Swimming in them with Rio was something she would always remember—something to cherish. But her nerves were stretching to breaking point. Every joke they shared, every kiss, hug, touch, made her more conscious of the fact that she needed to tell him the truth.

He looked at her as though she was the most perfect specimen on earth. And even as she wondered why she couldn't find the words, she knew.

She didn't want him to stop.

She didn't want him to see her flaws.

And when he learned the truth, he would. It would change things. Would he even want to be with her once he knew who she was and why she'd lied?

She was breaking his cardinal rule and it was breaking her heart.

She fell asleep with the secret in her heart and Rio's arm around her. She fell asleep with no answers and very little hope.

CHAPTER ELEVEN

'WHY DO WE not spend some time on Arketà next?' he murmured, flipping the pages of a newspaper, his eyes resting on hers.

Tilly's pulse trembled like a guitar string being plucked. 'Your island?'

'My *other* island,' he said with a teasing smile.

'I told you—I have to get back,' she said, dropping her eyes to the table to shield her uncertainty from him.

'So? Next weekend, then.'

She shook her head, consternation drawing her brows together. 'I have something on,' she mumbled.

'What is it?'

'Just a thing.'

His expression was pleasant, but she could see the ice-like determination in his eyes. He was assessing her, as though she were a problem he needed to solve.

'Training for a mission to Mars?' he said with mock seriousness. 'Adopting a guide dog? Running in the marathon?'

Her smile was cursory. 'Just a thing. It's not a big deal.'

'So cancel it.' He shrugged, his eyes still hard and unyielding. 'I will have my plane collect you.'

'Your *plane*?' she said, and the chasm between them seemed to grow. 'You'll have your plane come and get me and take me to your island? Your *other* island?'

He was as rich as Croesus. And she was not. She was nothing like he thought. In the normal course of events they would never have crossed paths, and they'd never have become lovers. He was sleeping with Cressida, not Matilda.

Sharp spikes of feeling stabbed at her heart.

Cressida was the kind of woman he made a habit of dating. Cressida with her expensive jewellery and haute couture and luxury handbags and Bugatti Veyron and Cartier account.

Cressida with her VIP entry to any party around the world, with her private jet to match his, her penchant for rich, gorgeous men.

'Except for Marina, have you ever been in a serious relationship?' she asked jerkily, her eyes not meeting his.

He put the newspaper down on the table, his expression impatient. 'I have dated. Why do you ask?'

'I just…' She shook her head. 'Am I your type?'

He shook his head. 'I don't know if I have such a thing as a "type",' he said finally.

'But, I mean, you usually date women like me, right? Women who have trust funds and move in the same circles as you?'

'As *us*,' he said, with no idea of how the slight correction hurt. 'And, yes. *Naturalmente*.'

'Why *naturalmente*?'

He expelled a breath. 'What is this about, Cressida?'

'I'm just trying to understand you better,' she hedged quietly.

'I have never had a serious relationship,' he said through compressed lips. 'I have dated many women...'

'And by that you mean slept with?'

He dipped his head in acknowledgement. 'I date, yes, but primarily these relationships are about sex. For me and for them. I do not lie about my intentions, if this is what worries you.'

'No.' She shook her head, her throat thick and scratchy. She knew quite definitively where he came down on the whole honesty issue. 'Have you ever dated—slept with—someone who *didn't* have millions of pounds?'

He laughed, then, apparently finding the question ridiculous. 'I do not ask to inspect their bank statements at the door to my bedroom.'

Her cheeks flushed. 'I just mean someone *normal*.'

'I know what you mean, yet I do not understand why you're asking me this now.'

She forced a smile to her face. 'I'm just trying to understand you, that's all.'

He picked up the paper again, flicking a page abruptly. 'I do not find it easy to trust. Marina taught me well,' he said finally. 'I do not want to sleep with women who might have ulterior motives.'

She sucked in an indignant breath, shocked to imagine him ever thinking that of her. 'Just the ones you're using for sex?' she snapped back.

His confusion was obvious. 'Why are you so angry about this? I have casual sex with women, and yes, generally they're moneyed. So what? What does it matter?'

'It matters,' she said finally.

'Fine.' He closed the paper again. 'If you want to discuss our sex lives, let's come back to yours. You exercise no judgement in the men you take to your bed. Is that any better than *my* approach?'

Fury whipped through her. She scraped her chair back and glared at him—but, damn it, the tears that had been stinging her eyes for days fell from her lashes.

He narrowed his gaze, his expression shifting.

He swore darkly in his own language, staring at Tilly as she battled tears, and felt like a first-class moron.

She had been looking for reassurance that she was special, and instead he'd made her feel like the last in a long line of wealthy lovers. And then he'd basically called her a tart into the mix.

'How dare you?'

She was so beautiful, even when tears were staining her cheeks, sending little wobbles of moisture down her face. She dashed them away, and her chest heaved with the effort of breathing.

'You are not like the women I've been with. I have told you this. Money, background—none of this matters to me with you. It is *you* I have fallen in love with, Cressida. You. Cressida Wyndham. The last woman on earth I would have thought I had anything in common with, and you have dug your way into my heart.'

She sobbed again, her tears falling faster now.

He couldn't understand it. 'Please, do not cry,' he said softly. 'I don't want to argue.'

She sniffed, but nodded.

The future she had held such hopes for was looking almost impossible to grab.

He turned his attention back to the paper and pretended to read. Something was worrying her. Something he didn't understand and certainly couldn't help her with unless she chose to speak to him. She was on edge—like a cat on hot tin.

He turned the page again—and froze as his beautiful lover appeared before him, her head bent, dark sunglasses covering her eyes, and her hand held by a man with scruffy blond hair and a ring through his nose.

'Would you care to tell me how you can be in two places at once?' he heard himself ask, the question calm despite the volcanic lava hammering him from the inside out.

Across the table, Tilly froze too. Her eyes met his with a tangle of confusion and then slowly dropped to the newspaper.

Even upside down she could read the headline.

HEIRESS WEDS LOVER!
SECRET CEREMONY!
DETAILS HERE!

Her stomach swooped and she gripped the table for strength.

Her eyes were enormous in her face as he lifted the page and she skimmed the first bold paragraph.

Shock and a thousand questions slammed into her. The press were always printing outrageous stories about the somewhat outlandish heiress. Surely this was just another? It couldn't be true.

Her eyes dropped to Cressida's hand; an enormous diamond ring glinted from her finger.

She'd married *him*? Ewan Rieu-Bailee, the man she'd been tangled with earlier in the summer?

Rumours weren't fact, and yet the picture was pretty damning.

As was the look Rio had for Tilly.

She darted a tongue out, moistening her lips. 'That's not me.'

'Obviously,' he said sarcastically, still staring at her.

It was a look that spoke volumes. It said everything she had been shouting at herself. Confusion, disapproval, anger, mistrust.

'She married him…'

Tilly thought back to their conversation. *'I have a wedding to go to. And Daddy would never approve.'*

Her own wedding?

Her heart turned over as she thought of Art Wyndham and how furious he'd be. And Tilly had unwittingly played a part in the whole thing! She would never knowingly hurt her boss—she adored him. And yet she'd been a crucial instrument in allowing Cressida to skive off and get married, with the whole world none the wiser.

'Oh, God,' she groaned, squeezing her eyes shut, no longer able to meet the full force of his interrogating glare. 'I had no idea.'

'You are not Cressida Wyndham.'

Though he hadn't spoken them particularly loudly, the words reverberated through the small cabin with the force of furious bullets.

'Who are you?'

'I…' She stared at the picture and the world collapsed around her.

'Who *are* you?' Now he shouted, his temper impossible to contain. He scraped his chair back so that he was standing, staring at her as if she'd sprouted four heads.

Tilly was shaking, her whole body quivering. She propped herself on the table, needing strength and support.

'Who the hell *are* you?'

'I'm… I'm the same person you fell in love with. My name is different, that's all.'

'You have been lying to me. You have been in my bed, in my arms, and I know nothing about you.'

'You know *everything* about me,' she whispered, reaching out and curling her fingers around his forearm. 'I'm not Cressida, but I'm still me.'

'And who is *that*?' he demanded, his eyes narrowed, his expression grim.

'I'm…'

Nausea was a wave and she was surfing it unrelentingly, occasionally dipping beneath the surface to the point when she thought she might vomit.

'My name is Tilly. Matilda. I work for Art Wyndham.'

His eyes, so grey when he was in a state of passion, almost blue when he laughed, were dark now, like a bleak, storm-ravaged night.

'Did Art set this up? What possible purpose could he have for sending you here?'

'No,' she whispered, her pulse thready as she denied the older man's involvement in this.

But Rio was jumping two steps ahead. 'Was he

hoping I'd drop the price if you asked it of me? That the inducement of you in my bed would be some kind of a bargaining chip?'

'No—no!' She shook her head violently, repulsed by even the suggestion. 'He doesn't know. It's… Cressida asked me…we're so alike, you see.'

He stared down at the picture. The woman had long red hair like Cressida—no, like Matilda. Pale skin, and, yes, a wide mouth. But there were differences too. A thousand of them. Though perhaps not to the untrained eye. It was simply that he was the world expert in all things Cressida—no, *Matilda*.

'You lied to me.'

She nodded. That was undeniable, something she would always regret. But that didn't mean she couldn't make him understand her reasoning.

'I… I didn't even know you when I agreed to do this.'

His lips twisted in a cruel smile. 'You know me now, though, and still you have been lying to me. Why?'

She opened her mouth and closed it again, her eyes shifting to the paper. She stared at Cressida, and the sense of having been betrayed filled the room. Not just for Rio, but for Tilly, too.

Cressida had used her.

Tilly had provided cover for Cressida to do something Tilly would never knowingly have been involved in. Her marriage to this man was a disaster. He'd already cheated on Cressida publicly, joked about getting her addicted to drugs… He was bad news. And now he was Mr Cressida Wyndham.

'Well, Matilda?' asked Rio, and the sound of her name on his lips did something odd to her heart.

It squeezed as though a band was being tightened around it. She had dreamed of him saying her name! But not like this. Not with derisive anger and disgust.

She no longer felt bound by secrecy. Cressida's news was in the papers; there was nothing left to protect.

Except herself.

The idea that she'd taken money so that Cressida could scamper off and marry a man no one in their right mind would approve of made Tilly feel dirty and mercenary. Rio was already looking at her as though she were filth on his shoe; how would he react if he knew she'd been paid? That this was a business deal for her, first and foremost—a chance to profit from a genetic twist of fate that had made her and Cressida twins that weren't related?

After so many lies, surely honesty had to be the way forward. She needed to trust him enough to tell him the truth. He'd said he loved her. That meant that he loved *all* of her. What was in a name?

'Who I am doesn't change what we are.' She moved to him with urgency and pressed her hands to his broad, strong chest. 'I lied about my name.' Her words were hoarse with urgency. 'Nothing else. *Nothing* else.'

Her fingers splayed wide and then his mouth was crushing down on hers with ferocious intensity. His hands pushed at her shoulders, tangling in her hair, and her heart skidded in her chest with a kind of relief she'd never imagined.

It was going to be okay.

This made sense.

She kissed him back and her fingers sought flesh,

pulling at his shirt and lifting it so she could run her fingers over his ridged abdomen.

His hands dragged over her sides and she ground her hips against him, needing him, needing to remind him of what they shared. It was a primal imperative, a certainty that she wouldn't allow him to forget.

Her mouth clashed with his in a fierce meshing of teeth, tongues and lips, angry and desperate. His mouth was demanding and she met his demands, explaining in that kiss that she was still the woman he loved.

He swore into her mouth—a guttural expression of his anger and darkness as he lifted her, hooked her legs around his hips and pushed her back against the wall. His weight held her captive.

She groaned and tasted salt. Sweat? No, tears. *Her* tears.

'I love you,' she promised him through her kisses and her tears, and he pulled away, his hands lifting her from the wall and carrying her through the cabin to his bedroom. The bedroom she'd woken in that morning, feeling that all was right in the world.

His expression was a hard mask of disbelief. He laid her down on the bed—not gently, but not roughly either, just matter-of-factly. Tilly had the sense that he was as focussed on her as he would be a competitor in the boardroom. There was determination in the steel glint of his eyes as he brought his mouth back to hers, as though he was weighing her strengths and weaknesses and developing a plan.

But, for Tilly, this was what she needed. He was angry, and she understood that, but still he wanted her—because he knew, deep down, that there was rightness in what they were. Was he angry at himself for wanting her even now?

He pushed out of his shorts and relief speared through her.

It would be okay. It couldn't *not* be.

His body was heavy on hers and his tongue insistent as it lashed hers. Her body responded in ways she couldn't control. Fires were spinning through her and she had no control to stop what was happening; she had no control over anything. She was at his whim and at his mercy, his for the taking for ever and ever. Did he realise that she was his? Utterly and always?

'I love you,' she said again, and the words were tumbling out of her. She needed him to understand. 'I didn't come here to lie to you. I didn't even know you'd be here.'

His expression showed impatience. Was he listening? Did he hear her? His fingers pulled at her panties and she stared up at him, then reached for his face, cupping his cheeks, holding him still.

'Look at me,' she said, with a voice that trembled and a heart that was hammering wildly. 'Look at me and tell me you don't know me,' she implored, her eyes scanning his face, willing him to remember what they were.

His grunt was impossible to interpret, but the pressing of his arousal at her core was everything she needed. She sobbed with dark desire—when they made love she would feel better. *He* would feel better. This just made sense.

'You want me?' he asked through gritted teeth, his hands trapping her wrists and pinning them out to her sides.

Tilly's face was covered in tears, her cheeks pink, her hair in disarray. There were scratches on her from his stubble; she was marked. She was his. But he needed her to say it. He needed her to surrender completely to him. Even then, would it be enough? To overlook her betrayal and manipulations?

'Yes,' she moaned, writhing, hot beneath him.

His smile held no humour; it was a twist of his lips. If Tilly had seen it she would have described it as cruel. But her eyes were shut. She was waiting for him to give her everything she needed, to remember that he loved her.

He thrust inside her and she cried out as relief exploded like fireworks in her blood.

'Yes!' she shouted again.

'Do you love me?' he demanded, pulling out.

His desertion was a physical ache low in her abdomen. She lifted her hips, trying to find him, to welcome him back but a muscle jerked in his cheek.

'You said you love me.'

'I do,' she groaned, her eyes clashing with his, begging him, silently communicating the truth of her heart.

He shook his head. 'I don't believe you.'

And he thrust into her again.

Her grief and shock were quickly pushed sideways by the desire that was rocking her. But they were there still, in the back of her mind, like little bombs of reality she couldn't detonate just yet.

She didn't realise that she was saying it over and over again. *'I love you, I love you, I love you...'* like an incantation that would wrap him up in the magic they'd created.

He swore in his own language and his mouth dropped to hers. He kissed the words angrily into her being, silencing her finally, leaving only the sound of their heavy breathing and the cracking whip of desire in the room.

Misery was there, on the edge of everything, but it couldn't stave off the pleasure that was climbing to a fever-pitch inside her, taking control of her body nerve by nerve until finally she catapulted over, sobbing and moaning as the crescendo of physical joy broke over her. He chased her, his body releasing itself in a guttural cry, his hands around her wrists loosening to push his body weight off her as soon as he'd exploded, so that he could look at her, rocked by the final throes of desire.

He stared at her with an intensity that she might have believed to be love if it hadn't instantly struck her heart cold.

'I will remember you like this,' he said bleakly, and before the last vestiges of pleasure had ebbed from her he was gone, pulling himself up to stand, turning his back on her. His shoulders moved with the rise and fall of his breathing.

Tilly stared at him and those little disastrous truths exploded now—terrors that filled her with pain. 'How can you doubt this?' she asked quietly, wiping her cheeks and noticing absentmindedly that his fingers had left red marks on the pale flesh of her wrists. They were fading already and she resented that. She didn't want to lose any physical markers of what they'd shared.

His laugh rang in the room like an accusation. 'I doubt *everything*!'

'You love me and I hurt you,' she said quietly.

'*Love* you? I don't even *know* you, Cressi— Damn it! Matilda. You are every bit as bad as Marina. No, you are worse! I actually loved you, and you allowed me to…to bare my soul to you even knowing how dishonest you were being.'

She winced and he spun to face her, his expression fury personified.

'You weren't supposed to be here,' she said, pushing up onto her elbows, her eyes imploring him to hear what she was saying. 'By the time I'd fallen in love with you and we were…*this*, it was too late.'

'Too late?' He jerked his head back as though she'd struck him. 'How many times could you have told me the truth?'

'I wanted to,' she whispered. 'But it wasn't my secret.'

He shook his head, his expression a mix of anger and mistrust. His hair was tousled and loose over his forehead. 'What we just did—*that* is the only truth we have shared this week.'

Her orgasm was still subsiding, her mind was fogged, and it took her a moment to hear his words and to make any kind of sense of them.

'Sex,' he supplied with dark determination.

A shiver ran the length of her spine.

'Don't say that,' she whispered. 'It's been so much more than just a physical thing. Think of every moment we've shared and tell me that it's been a lie.'

'Easily.' His smile was grim. 'It has been a lie. I thought you were someone else. Everything I thought about you was based on misinformation.'

'No!' She shook her head, but he continued.

'We've had sexual attraction and desire—incredible chemistry. But that's not something I can't get more of. And with someone who *won't* be dishonest with every word she breathes.'

Her breath hurt. The very idea of his supplanting her in his bed nauseated her.

'Rio,' she said softly, but the word was drenched in the tears that were streaming down her cheeks. 'I wanted to tell you. *So* many times. But I promised Cressida and...' She thought guiltily of the enormous sum Cressida had paid her. How could he forgive her? 'I *had* to honour that.'

'If you say so.'

His detachment hurt far more than the anger. It was so angry.

'Can you be ready in an hour?'

'For what?' Her skirt was ruched around her hips, and her hair was a bird's nest that spoke of passion and need.

'To get back to reality,' he said crisply. 'I want you off this damned island and out of my life.'

'Rafaelo will take you to Sorrento. My helicopter there will take you to Naples, where my jet is fuelled and waiting.'

'Rio...'

She stared at him, the change in his demeanour impossible to reconcile with the man she'd woken up beside. He'd showered after they'd made love. Only it hadn't been making love. Not for him. It had been making a point.

She swallowed, the taste of acid burning her throat. 'Please let me explain.'

He stood at the table, his hands gripping the back of a chair. His knuckles glowed white with tension.

'Do you think any explanation will fix this?'

She squeezed her eyes shut and nodded.

'Veramente?' he demanded. 'I know nothing about you, Matilda Morgan who works for Art Wyndham, but you know *everything* about me. Things I have never spoken to another soul I have told you this week. You *know* me. Surely you know I could never forgive this deception?'

'I didn't set out to deceive you,' she said quickly.

'What does that matter? The result is the same, whether you planned it or not. And you chose to deceive me even when you knew what we were becoming.' He shook his head. 'What I *thought* we were becoming,' he corrected with cruel derision in his words.

She sucked in a deep breath. She *had* to make him understand.

'I have a brother,' she said firmly, her eyes holding his even as the withering uninterest in his made her gut churn. 'Jack. He's my twin. We've always been close. And he got into trouble recently.'

She paused here. She had made a habit of concealing Jack's failings from the world out of a need to protect him. But even that had to be sacrificed for any hope with Rio.

'Do not misunderstand me. I do not *wish* to know you,' he said coldly. 'Rather, I know all I need to know about you.'

'Please,' she said thickly. 'Let me tell you this.'

He flicked a lazy glance at his watch. 'Rafaelo will be here any minute. You have until he arrives.'

Urgency made her speak faster, louder. 'Jack owed money to some guys—bad guys—and at the same time Cressida asked me to come here and pretend to be her. She would pay me to come here as her.' She darted her tongue out and licked her lower lip. 'I was very worried about Jack, and then all of a sudden there was this perfect solution.'

Her eyes met his and then darted away, scared by the Arctic hatred she saw there.

'Why would you think this a solution? Impersonating someone is not easy.'

'I've done it before,' she muttered, staring at the floor. 'Not ever for as long as this. It started with a party she didn't want to go to, and then there was a film premiere. Sometimes she's asked me to leave a restaurant before her so that the press think she's gone.'

'And she *pays* you for this?'

Tilly nodded. 'But that's not why I do it.'

His laugh was a scoff. 'I see. I presume you do it because you get some kind of psychopathic kick out of lying to people?'

She shook her head. 'I feel sorry for her,' Tilly whispered the words. 'She's not a bad person, Rio. Just selfish and spoiled. But she...she deserves better than the treatment she gets in the press.'

He made a noise of disagreement.

'You weren't meant to be here. I thought I'd meet an estate agent, get a tour of the island and then...'

The words dwindled away as embarrassment over her naivety swallowed her.

'And then what? Take payment for the deception? Fix your brother's problems? Go back to your life, having lied to your boss?' He shook his head. 'None of this is making you look any better to me.'

She nodded, her throat raw. 'I didn't know she was going to get married. I would never have taken part in this if I had.'

He didn't respond, and for a second she hoped that maybe she was getting through to him. But one look at his features, set in a mask of stone, and she was absolutely sure that she'd lost him for good.

'How much?' he asked with a thick accusation.

She didn't pretend to misunderstand. 'Thirty thousand pounds.'

His eyes swooped closed on the information as he digested it. She had no idea what he was thinking. In the distance she heard the unmistakable sound of the speedboat and panic slammed into her.

'I love you,' she said quietly, with complete honesty.

His eyes snapped open. 'Another lie,' he ground out. 'Where is your bag?'

'Not a lie,' she insisted, walking around the table and putting a hand on his arm.

He stared at it as though she was wiping butter all over him. His gaze met hers with challenge.

'I don't want to leave you,' she said thickly. 'Let me stay.'

His eyes flashed with a dark emotion she couldn't understand.

'You want to stay?' he murmured.

Hope soared inside her. She nodded.

'You can stay, *cara*. But you should know that all I will ever want you for is sex. It is the only part of this that I believe you weren't faking. I'll even throw thirty thousand pounds into the mix if that makes you feel more comfortable.'

It took several aching seconds for the implication of his words to sink in.

Never in his life had he seen such visceral pain cross the features of someone's face. No matter how furious he was with her, how much he loathed her in that moment, seeing his words hit their target left him with a hollow feeling in his chest. All the colour had drained from her flesh and tears had sprung to her eyes.

When she lifted a hand to slap his cheek he made no effort to stop her.

It seemed like the perfect end to what they had been.

'I'll take that as a no,' he said, the words blank of any emotion.

'Take it as a go to hell.'

CHAPTER TWELVE

THE ELEVATOR WAS SLOW.

Or perhaps Rio was just impatient.

Not that he conveyed a hint of emotion.

His eyes were like steel as they stared straight ahead, his expression set.

Would she be surprised to see him?

His smile was tight and humourless. He had deliberately avoided making an appointment so that he didn't tip her off. When he saw Matilda Morgan again he wanted it to be with the edge of surprise.

He flicked a glance at his wristwatch, noting the time with dispassionate interest. He'd chosen to arrive in the late afternoon, knowing the chances of Tilly still being away from her desk at lunch were slight.

The metallic doors of the lift pinged open and he strode out of the lift with no concept of the heads that lifted as passed. Speculative glances, some recognition, a lot of interest.

A bank of three receptionists sat in the centre of the tiled foyer. He paused in front of one of them, employing a banal, non-committal smile. 'Art Wyndham.'

The woman curled her manicured fingers over the

felt end of her telephone headset. 'Is Mr Wyndham expecting you, sir?'

'No.' He smiled again, and saw the effect it had on her. 'But he won't want to miss me.'

The woman stared at him for a moment too long and then returned her attention to the computer screen.

She checked a diary and then went to press a button on the phone, but Rio shook his head. 'I'd prefer to surprise him.'

'Oh...'

Perhaps the receptionist should have employed more care, but she was face to face with Rio Mastrangelo and any powers of thought and reason had deserted her.

She nodded. 'You'll need to go up one more level. His PA's desk is just outside the lift. She'll direct you.'

'*Grazie.*' He spun on his heel, stalking back to the lift and pressing the 'up' button. It appeared immediately, of course. That was how things generally worked for Rio.

The ride up took seconds.

He stood, a study in nonchalance, and waited for the doors.

They slid open silently and his eyes immediately moved to the desk. As promised, it was directly in front of the elevator, though halfway across the floor. A woman's head was bent. A dark head.

He frowned. Had she changed her hair? Disappointment fired in his gut. Her hair had been spectacular.

Time seemed to stand still as Tilly's head lifted and he waited for her eyes to meet his.

He frowned.

She was not Matilda.

He recovered quickly. He'd come to see Art, not Matilda. What did it matter that she wasn't at her desk?

'Is Art free?' he asked, his tone clipped, his words impatient.

'Oh….um…' She stared down at her desk and then reached for her phone, dropping it once before shaking her head and lifting it to her ear.

'Mr Wyndham?' she said, and then bit down on her lip shamefacedly as she pressed a button. 'Mr Wyndham?' she tried again. 'There's a man here to see you.'

The woman was quiet for a moment, nodding, and then she lifted her eyes to Rio's face. 'What's your name?'

Rio's lips curled in a small smile of disapproval. This woman wouldn't have lasted two hours in *his* employ. 'Rio Mastrangelo,' he offered.

She'd obviously heard of him. 'Oh! *Oh!* It's Mr Mastrangelo, sir!' Another pause. 'Right away.'

She put the phone down and smiled brightly. 'His office is the second door on the right.'

Confident that the usual form would have been for her to lead him there, and to offer refreshment, Rio nodded in a terse acknowledgement and strode across the floor.

'Rio!' Art pulled the door inwards, sending a bemused look down the hallway at his PA. 'Come in.'

Rio stepped into the office, barely noting the luxurious surrounds.

'You'll have to forgive the temp. Nice enough girl,

but what she knows about administration you could fit on the back of a postcard.'

Art waved a hand at the comfortable leather sofas near the enormous windows that painted an expansive view of the Thames.

Rio sat, crossing one ankle over his knee.

'I had to fire my assistant,' Art grumbled. 'Though, having spent the last four weeks getting intimately acquainted with the dregs of every temp agency in the city, I almost wish I hadn't.'

Rio didn't want to analyse the emotional response he was having to this discovery. 'You fired Matilda?'

Art narrowed his eyes, putting two and two together with less efficiency than Rio would have liked.

'That's right,' he murmured. 'You met her. Or rather you met her in the guise of my daughter.' He spat out the summation with deep condemnation. 'Sorry about that. Of course I had no idea what they were up to.'

'Of course.' Rio nodded, his mind poring over this fact. 'When?'

Art looked confused. 'When, what?'

'When did you fire her?'

'As soon as she got back. I can't believe she helped Cressida marry that useless waste-of-space *artist*.' He shouted the last word as if it were the worst thing a man could be. 'Anyway, that's not your concern. What can I do you for?'

The pounding wouldn't stop. The pounding in her head and then, making it worse, the pounding at the door.

'I'm coming,' she called, wincing as the words shredded her raw throat.

She grabbed a tissue as she passed the nightstand and blew her nose, then discarded the white paper on the floor. She pushed her hair back from her face, tangling her fingers in knots. When had she last showered? Days ago, she thought with a frown, hating the idea of standing upright for any period of time.

A sneeze burst from her and it was like being slapped over the head with a hammer. She pulled the door inwards and the sneeze was quickly followed by a second, then a third, so that she was disorientated when she blinked her eyes open.

It was early evening, and the sky was dark. Surely that explained why she wasn't seeing properly?

Confusion followed disorientation. Was she hallucinating? Or was Rio Mastrangelo really standing on her front doorstep looking better than anyone had a right to?

Gone was the coarse hair that had covered his chin and upper lip in a mask of stubble. He had shaved, and his hair was neat—not a hint of Island Rio remained in evidence. But it was him, all right, nonchalant and sexy in a slate-grey suit with a crisp white shirt open at the collar to reveal the thick column of his neck. A neck she had loved to kiss and bite and taste.

She swallowed and looked away quickly. Stars burst at her temple too fast. Her eyes had been sore for days.

'What are you doing here?'

'*Dio*. You look like death warmed up.'

She groaned inwardly, keeping her fingers gripping tightly to the door. He was right. She hadn't just been skipping showers, but meals and hair-washing, and she was pretty sure she'd spilled some coffee down the front of her cream shirt, leaving a tell-tale trail of caramel staining.

Still, that was no business of his. He hadn't even walked her to the door of the cabin when Rafaelo had knocked. She'd walked away from him, head held high, and she stood before him now with her shoulders squared. 'Did you come to insult me a little more?'

'Have you been crying?' he asked with incredulity.

As if she hadn't had every *reason* to cry! The first two weeks back from Prim'amore had been strewn with tears. Not just tears over losing Rio, but tears over the injustice of losing her job and the friendship with Art that she had foolishly believed mattered as much to the older man as it had to her.

'No.' She sneezed emphatically, her head spinning with the jerk of movement, and he took advantage of her distraction to move closer, lifting a hand to the door.

'What are you doing?' she demanded, the words thick with congestion.

He frowned. 'You are ill?'

'I have a cold.' She kept her hand on the door even as he went to move it inwards.

'A cold?' he repeated, his frown deepening.

She coughed. 'Yes. You know—sneezing. Coughing. Sore throat.' As if to emphasise her point, she sneezed again.

'It's summer.'

Her eyes narrowed. 'So?'

He expelled a deep breath. 'Then get inside and sit down before you fall down.'

Tilly feared his prediction was not an unlikely one.

Her head was woozy and thick, her body shivering. 'I will—as soon as you go.'

He took the final step so he was level with her—though he towered over her, in point of fact, his strong body so close she could feel his warmth and smell his spicy fragrance. His nearness was intoxicating and overpowering, and her already ravaged senses weren't up to fending off the kick of desire that surged inside her.

It surprised her.

It was wholly unwanted.

And it weakened her too, so that when he pushed at the door again it gave easily.

She didn't resist. She did move back, though, putting distance between herself and Rio.

He stepped into her home, his eyes glittering in his handsome face as they bored into her for a long moment and then moved down the hallway, studying the pictures on her walls and the arrangements of tulips that were wilting now, their water emitting a faintly rancid odour. Or at least she imagined it was, judging by from the brown sludge outline on the glass vase. Her nose was too blocked to fully appreciate it.

Strangely, though, Rio tickled every one of her senses, even though she was barely functioning.

'What are you doing here?' she asked, focussing on a point over his shoulder. Surreptitiously she pressed her back against the wall, needing the support to stay upright.

A muscle jerked in his jaw. 'Where is your bedroom?'

Stricken, she shook her head. 'What? You can't be serious?'

He looked at her as though she'd taken leave of her senses. 'As hard as I find it to resist you,' he said with a hint of droll amusement, 'you look like you are about to faint. Go and sleep. I will make you tea.'

'Tea,' she repeated, confusion making her eyes crinkle.

'Go. Lie down.'

'No. Rio, I'm… I do need to…to rest. But please,' she said with a quiet stoicism that came from the heart, 'don't make me tea.'

She lifted a hand, because she couldn't not touch him, and pressed her fingers into his chest. Electricity arced between them, but this time it burned her. It wasn't just an arc of desire; it was an explosion.

She dropped her hand away quickly and swallowed. 'I don't know why you're here, but I want you to go away again.'

The words rang with palpable grief.

'Go to sleep,' he said with a small nod.

She sighed, reaching for the wall for support. He was going to go. Whatever had brought him to her home, it wasn't important enough for him to fight for it.

'Goodbye,' she said, and it was only as she reached her bedroom that she realised he had said nothing back.

It was early in the morning when she woke. Not yet dawn, the sky was just yielding its black finality to the hint of daylight, negotiating the terms of their treaty with leaden grey and pale pink.

She sat up without sneezing or grabbing her head for the first time in over a week. She lifted a hand to her hair, pulling it over her shoulder in one big tangle of red. She ran her fingers over its length. It was a tangled bird's nest, and for the first time since getting sick she found the idea of washing it didn't leave her feeling exhausted.

She coughed. It didn't feel as though her throat had been slashed with razor blades.

But it wasn't until she'd started the shower running and stripped her three-day-old outfit from her body that she remembered Rio's visit the evening before. Had it been a dream? What reason could he have had for coming to see her in real life? Their business was over. More than over.

It was broken beyond repair.

Had she dreamed his visit? Lord knew she'd had enough dreams of Rio Mastrangelo for that theory to be utterly plausible. She looked down at her fingertips, trying to remember the sensation of touching him. She'd pressed her hand against his chest.

And she frowned.

He'd been clean-shaven. It was easier to imagine him as the formidable tycoon when he looked like that, instead of the island version of himself.

She lathered her hair and rinsed it, then conditioned it and soaped her whole body, propping her back against the tiles when a wave of tiredness returned.

This cold had been dogging her steps for well over a week. At first she'd thought it was just exhaustion, but then her ears had begun to ache, her throat to sting, her eyes to scratch, and finally she'd suc-

cumbed to the sickness. In some ways it had been a
relief. A physical justification for her pervasive sense
of misery.

It had allowed to her to climb wearily into bed.

To stay there.

To hide under her duvet and let the world roll past,
carrying on without her contribution.

Strength was in her now, though. She'd slept sol-
idly, as though seeing Rio had given her some kind
of closure.

Closure? *As if.*

Her heart twisted with a pain she was becoming
used to.

She flicked the water off and grabbed a towel,
wrapping it around her body and then aggressively
drying her hair. She felt much better, but there was
still an exhaustion within her that came from having
not eaten properly in days.

She didn't bother to dress. Instead she cinched
her silk robe around her waist and pulled the door
inwards, padding down the hall. The scent of decay-
ing flowers assailed her and, as she'd suspected, it
was disgusting. She curled her fingers around the
vase, lifting it and carrying it with her to the kitchen.

As she cut through her small, cheery lounge, with
its white fabric sofa and colourful throw cushions, its
view of her small courtyard, she froze.

Rio sat amongst the cushions on her sofa, his body
still, in a seated position, his head bent over the coffee table. He wore the same clothes as he had the
day before, though at some point in the night he'd
discarded his coat. It hung on one of the chairs that
were perched at the window.

She was so shocked she almost dropped the vase.

'What are you doing here?' she demanded, even as her body screamed at her to go to him, to close the distance and straddle him.

Her body begged her to give in to her craving but her mind was rejecting that idea wholesale.

He didn't want her.

'You can stay, cara. Stay. But you should know that all I will ever want you for is sex. It is the only part of us that I believe you weren't faking. I'd even throw thirty thousand pounds into the mix if that made you feel more comfortable.'

He turned to look at her, his eyes probing hers before dropping, performing a cursory inspection of her figure.

'I asked what you're doing here,' she said through gritted teeth.

He stood then, skirting around the sofa and crossing to stand right in front of her. He reached out, and for one thrilling, confusing second she thought he was going to hug her. But instead his hands took the vase from her.

'Before you drop it on your feet,' he explained with a tight smile.

She didn't return the smile. 'Rio.' It was a warning. Though it was only one word, it showed how close she was to breaking point. It was both a plea and a closed door.

He compressed his lips; they were a line in his handsome face. More handsome now that she could see the hard angles of his cheeks, the cleft of his chin. She swallowed convulsively and looked away. Morning sun dappled the windows.

He turned and stalked towards the kitchen. Confused enough to be curious, she followed. He held the gloopy flowers around their stems as he tipped the water down the sink, then lifted them out and dropped them into the bin.

There were two coffee cups at the side of the sink and a plate that held crumbs. He'd eaten? Toast?

He was looking at her, and it was a look that penetrated her soul.

When he spoke, the words were quiet and husky with emotion. 'You look better.'

She took it as an assessment of her health rather than as a compliment. Her skin was pale, her eyes red-rimmed, her hair still wet. 'Thanks.'

His mouth twisted.

'This is you?'

He pointed to the fridge and one of the many photos she had taped across its bland white front.

Her eyes slid sideways, taking in the old family photo he'd pointed to. It had been taken around the time she and Jack had finished secondary school. She'd been in a full-blown *Sex and the City* phase and was wearing a fabric flower hooked into her shirt that even Carrie Bradshaw would have called excessive, with lace pink and white petals. Her parents sat as their bookends, proud smiles on their faces.

'Yeah.'

'Your brother?'

'My twin.'

He nodded, filing the information away. 'You don't look alike.'

'No.' She reached up a hand to her hair, tugging

at its damp red length. 'He got Dad's colouring; I got Mum's.'

Rio was in her kitchen, and the strange thing was she felt an overwhelming sense that he belonged. It was unnerving in the extreme.

He turned away, reaching for two more cups and hooking one under the coffee machine spout. He fed a pod into the top and pressed the button. The noise was reminiscent of his machine on Prim'amore.

It sent shivers down her spine.

Fragments of the last time they'd seen each other were like sharp glass, cutting through her equilibrium. The way he'd refused to listen to her, refused to let her even try to explain. The way he'd seen only the worst in her actions.

Time away from him had dragged anger towards bewilderment. How *dared* he think he'd loved her when he'd found it so easy to turn his back and walk away? No, push her away even as she'd been begging to stay.

'What are you doing here?' She spoke with a steely determination that replicated his the last time they'd spoken.

'I went to see Wyndham last night. You weren't there.'

Mortification at having lost her job—and having this man discover the fact—caused her stomach to flip. She lowered her gaze, but couldn't hide the bright red that bloomed in her cheeks.

'He fired you.'

Her eyes flared wide; but what was the point in lying? Spurred on to the defensive, she snapped sarcastically, 'Did he? I hadn't realised.'

A muscle jerked in Rio's cheek. Her eyes dropped to it of their own accord.

'I do not think he can fire you because you took a week off work.'

'That's not why—'

'There are laws to protect employees,' he said quietly, overriding her explanation.

She nodded, moving around him, skirting him at a safe distance, lifting the coffee cup out from the machine. He might be a guest in her home—albeit an uninvited one—but she was desperate for food and energy. She lifted the cup and inhaled its delicious scent gratefully.

'I know that. But...' She lifted her slender shoulders, unconscious of the way her robe gaped a little at the chest. 'I like him too much to fight it. I couldn't work for him now anyway. Not knowing what I'd helped orchestrate.'

Rio's eyes were watchful. 'Correct me if I'm wrong, but you had no idea Cressida was going to get married.'

'It doesn't matter.' She bit down on her lip and forced herself to meet his gaze. It would be over soon. 'I let her pay me to impersonate her. I lied to Art—a man I care for and admire beyond words. I lied to you, Rio. To *you*, the man I loved. And I'm lying to my parents now—it would kill them if they knew I'd been frogmarched out of the building by Security. That I'd been fired.'

Mortification crept along her skin at the surreal indignity she'd suffered. Strangely, she saw a corresponding anger in his expression. Had he come here to enjoy her failure? To show her how deserving she was of such humiliation?

'In any event,' she said quietly, 'none of that is your concern.'

He lifted his lip in a small flicker of a smile.

'Isn't it?'

His eyes were drawn to her face as if by an invisible magnet. He stared at her for so long that she shifted self-consciously, moving away from the coffee machine to the other side of the kitchen. She propped herself against the door, pretending fascination with the rim of her coffee cup.

'I didn't have your address,' he said quietly.

The sentence was strange. Discordant.

'The fact you're here disputes that,' she pointed out, sipping her coffee so fast she burned her throat a little.

He ignored the comment. 'Nor did I have your phone number. When you left the island—'

'After you *ordered* me to leave,' she felt obliged to remind him.

'I seem to remember giving you the option to remain,' he said, and the words were heavy with an emotion she couldn't identify. Anger? Annoyance? Irritation?

'As your paid lover?' she muttered, her stomach squeezing painfully at the recollection.

To her embarrassment, more tears drenched her eyes. She dug the nails of one hand into her palm, refusing to let them fall. Refusing to let him see her sadness.

'I was very angry,' he said, but it was not an apology and she noticed that.

'I know.'

She sipped her coffee and then turned away, walking with her spine straight and shoulders squared to the lounge. She sat on one of the dining chairs, though mistakenly chose the one with his jacket on it, so a very faint hint of *him* reached her, making her crave him so badly she felt as if she'd been punched low in the abdomen.

She cradled her coffee, taking warmth from it.

'I had thought love to be a construct, and then I met you and I lost myself completely. Discovering that it had all been an act of pretence for you...' He pulled a face. 'My pride was hurt. I lashed out.'

She swallowed. 'You had every right to be angry,' she murmured softly. 'I never thought I would meet *you*. I certainly didn't plan to...to feel like that. I wanted not to. I wanted to be able to ignore it.'

'Neither of us could ignore it,' he said with grim honesty.

'It doesn't matter now.' Her mouth lifted in what she seemed to remember was a smile. It felt incredibly strange on her face: heavy and tight.

'It matters to me,' he said, the lines of his body rigid. 'I came here today to apologise, Matilda.'

She closed her eyes. Her name—her real name—on his lips was heaven. But the knowledge that all this was coming to an end was an answering degree of agony.

'What for?'

'Take your pick,' he said, with a rueful smile that was belied by the self-disgust in his eyes. 'Suggesting you prostitute yourself to me. Telling you that all we'd shared was sex. Forcing you off my island even when every bone in my body wanted me to beg you to stay.'

Her eyes lifted to his, clashing with their grey depths in confusion.

He moved towards her now, and finally crouched at her feet. 'For telling you I loved you and then proving myself unworthy of your love in every way.'

He didn't touch her, but he was close, and just having him near her was sending goosebumps over her flesh.

'For leaving you to face all this alone, when I should have been standing beside you? For showing that I didn't support you even after I'd promised you with every kiss and every moment that I would?'

Her heart was racing but it was agony, each beat like a tiny blade pressing into her ribs. She felt it scratch and her breath burned in her lungs.

'You were angry,' she said again. 'But you need to know that the woman you met on the island...the one you said you loved...that was me. All I lied about was my name.'

He nodded. 'I know that.'

She froze. The three words brought her an exquisite sense of confusion. *He knew that?* What did that mean?

'I think I knew it even as I was telling you to go.'

He lifted a hand and rubbed it over her knee, as though he could scarcely believe it possible.

'I went to Prim'amore to deal with my own demons. I thought I had. But then there was so much anger—anger about my mother, my father, their choices and their lives—and I took it out on you. That was wrong of me.'

She flashed her eyes to his, but looked back at her coffee instantly.

His voice was insistent. 'Because *you*, Matilda Morgan, are the love of my life, and you deserved so much better than that. I should have stood shoulder to shoulder with you, listened to you and told you that I didn't care. That nothing you could do would change the facts. That I'd fallen in love with a coffee-addicted, clumsy, teetotal book-lover, and that I wanted to love her for ever. I want to love *you* for ever.' He cleared his throat. 'I will anyway, regardless of what you say. But, *cara*, I beg you to let me love you.' He groaned. 'Give me another chance to love you as you deserve.'

The words didn't make sense.

Nothing about this did.

She shook her head, her eyes huge in her face.

Was she hallucinating? Heaven knew she'd been sick enough and Rio-obsessed enough to be imagining this.

'I had no way of contacting you,' he admitted, the words gravelly. 'And I fought with myself for a long time. I stayed on the island and told myself again and again that I was glad you were gone. But every night I would reach for you, needing you.'

'That's just sex,' she intoned flatly, her heart thumping achingly. 'Like you said.'

'*No,*' he denied quickly, as though his life depended on her understanding. 'It was never just sex. I've done that. I know the difference.'

Great—just what she needed. A reminder of his virility and the way he'd indulged it with other women.

'I told myself I'd come to London to see Art, but really I should have known it was all about you. I wasn't sure you'd want to speak to me after the things I'd said and the way I'd behaved. I had a whole plan worked out, to make it impossible for you to ignore me, but then you weren't there.'

'What plan?' she asked, lifting her coffee to her lips and sipping it slowly while her mind worked even more slowly.

'To surprise you at your desk. To tell you I was meeting with Art to let him know that I can never sell Prim'amore after what it has come to mean to me. That I plan to build the house my mother designed and live in it with the woman I love. That I want to wake up every morning to the sound of you making coffee and turning the pages of your book. That I want to swim through the caves with you by my side, that I will build you your very own stairway into the volcano so that you can swim in its depths any time you wish. That the island is our home—that I believe it was our home from that very first night.'

A sob bubbled inside her chest and she dug her nails into her palms again, trying to quell it.

'But you weren't there, and when I heard you had been fired I felt guilt and despair in measures I have never known. I didn't protect you. I left you to face the firing squad.'

'It wasn't your job to protect me,' she said with stoic determination.

'No, but it is my privilege to *want* to,' he corrected quietly. 'I had arrogantly assumed you would be there, waiting for me to make my grand gesture and sweep you off your feet.'

'I would have quit if he hadn't fired me,' she said with a small shake of her head. 'I betrayed him.'

'You were trying to do a favour for Cressida,' he pointed out. 'You weren't to know she was using you so that she could marry that dropkick.'

Tilly swallowed. 'Anyway,' she said softly, her heart and mind fogged from all that he'd said, unsure how to proceed, 'it's done.'

'How is your brother?' he asked.

She started, shifting her eyes to his. 'I... He's okay,' she said, though she was guilty there too, for she had been so caught up with her own sadness that she'd barely checked in with Jack.

'Matilda?' he said, and she pulled a face.

'Tilly, please. The only time I'm called Matilda is when my parents are really, really angry with me.'

His smile flickered but it was reserved; uncertainty sat heavily around his shoulders. 'Tilly,' he said, the word low and deep.

Her nerves clenched.

'I was angry with you, and yet I am so lucky. I get to fall in love with you not once, but twice.'

She looked at him in confusion.

'The woman I met on the island, whom I loved instantly and completely—the woman who opened her heart to me and buried herself deep in mine. And now you and everything about you I don't yet know. Who are your family? What are your dreams? I want to know, and I want to love all of you. Will you let me?'

She let out a small sound. A sob? A laugh? She couldn't have determined, but it was accompanied by a watery smile and a nod of her head.

'I didn't want to lie to you,' she whispered. 'As soon as I knew how serious we were I wanted to tell you, but there was the money and… It all happened so fast.'

'I know this,' he said, stroking her hair. 'Tilly, I am sorry you lost your job. And if it's any consolation I believe Art would welcome you back with a flowery speech that would even outdo me.' He grinned.

She smiled. 'His is not an easy office to run.'

'I can imagine.' Rio nodded. 'But, as you are not working now, perhaps you would consider coming with me. Now. Tonight.'

'Coming with you where?'

His smile spread across his face like butter on warm toast. 'Into our future, *mi amore.*'

'You never told me how Art took the news?' Tilly murmured, her eyes trained on the water, looking for the first sign of Prim'amore.

He squeezed her hand and she looked up at him, her heart tripping over itself with its spasming response to the love in his eyes.

'I softened the blow a bit.'

She lifted a brow, waiting for him to continue.

'Arketà,' he explained. 'Why do I need *two* islands?'

Her smile was broad. 'You sold him your island?'

'I have it on good authority that two is excessive.' He grinned. 'It is a much better buy for him. It already has infrastructure and it is an easier commute to the mainland.'

'That was kind of you,' she said, but embarrassment at the unceremonious way she'd been dumped from her job still made her cringe.

Rio understood. 'When you are ready, we will visit

him together. He was wrong to fire you, and even more wrong to blame you for his daughter's duplicity. I believe he is aware of that, and regrets his actions.'

She shrugged, her eyes turning back to the water, seeking the island. 'I worked for him a long time. I really came to care for him. It's strange to think that he blamed me... And yet without me it would have been a lot more difficult for Cressida to run off and get married.'

'Do you think that would have stopped her?'

Tilly lifted her eyes to his, her expression thoughtful. 'No,' she said finally, shaking her head. 'When Cressida wants something, nothing will stand in her way.'

'Speaking of weddings...' He changed the subject subtly. 'I thought we could marry on the island. But, on reflection, this presents two problems.'

She jerked her head to his, her eyes showing that she didn't completely understand. 'Marry?'

'Our wedding,' he said with a nod, as though it were a foregone conclusion.

She laughed. In the two days since he'd arrived at her apartment they'd barely been separated. But she was pretty sure she hadn't missed a discussion about getting married.

'Did I sleep through a proposal?'

He blinked rapidly. 'I told you, didn't I? That I want to love you for ever?'

She laughed. 'Yes.'

'What did you think that meant?'

'I... That you love me?' she replied with a shake of her head.

'I said I would love you for ever, and I asked you

to let me love you,' he said, his lips twitching at the corners. 'Is that not a proposal and an acceptance?'

She tilted her head to the side. 'I don't recall a bended knee.'

'I do,' he grinned. 'I was crouched at your feet, wasn't I?'

She slapped a hand to her forehead, her cheeks hurting from smiling so widely. And behind his shoulder she saw the tip of the volcano crest above the ocean, and then, rapidly, the island.

Rafaelo turned the boat sharply, pushing it around into the cove that housed the cabin.

She let her eyes drift back to Rio's face and saw he was watching her.

'We'll see,' she said with another laugh, too enthralled by being back at the island to give the conversation her full attention.

As the boat slowed into the shallows Rio stood, moving to the back and pressing a button to let the anchor down. It made a mechanised noise as it began to drop, and then Rio leaped from the boat, landing with confident ease in the shallows of the ocean.

He lifted a hand up to Tilly, and she looked at it for a brief moment before jumping overboard, happily landing on her feet before dropping into the water, grinning from ear to ear as the water wrapped her, fully clothed, in its depths.

When she stood, he was looking at her as though she lost her mind—and he loved it. 'You are utterly unique,' he said with a shake of his head.

On the boat, Rafaelo cackled softly. Tilly winked at him and then jumped up, pushing at Rio's chest until he fell backwards into the water.

He laughed as he splashed to the ground. 'Why do I think life with you is going to leave very few dull moments?'

'If any,' she agreed with a nod.

He stood, shaking his head and reaching down to scoop her up. And she let him carry her out of the water towards the beach. He deposited her wet feet on the sand and then paced back to the boat, taking their two small bags and carrying them easily towards her.

She watched him, her heart soaring. Behind him the sun was dipping down, and everything was right in the world.

'Let me stow these inside,' he said.

She nodded, tears of happiness clogging her throat. She waved at Rafaelo as he turned the boat back out to sea and found a path just to the left of the sun's golden trail.

When Rio returned, it was with an ice-cold bottle of champagne and two glasses.

'After last time?' she said with a rueful smile.

'A small glass,' he said. 'I feel like celebrating.'

'And what are we celebrating?' she asked rhetorically, because fate and destiny had conspired to bring them every good thing in life.

He crouched down, so that he could better pop the champagne cork, but before he'd taken the foil from the top he reached for her hand.

'I think you missed my proposal earlier. So let me ask you now, Matilda Morgan, if you will marry me? Marry me anywhere, any time, but be my wife for always. I want to save you from falling into volcanoes for the rest of our days.'

She turned to look down at him and saw, for the

first time, that he was holding a small velvet box. And it was saturated. Her cheeks flushed as she realised he must have had it with him when she'd ploughed him into the ocean.

'Oh…' She blinked, almost blinded by the solitaire diamond. It was surrounded by a circlet of green stones.

'Like your eyes.'

The words were a love song all on their own. She felt the rhythm and verse move over her and her heart danced.

'I love it,' she promised.

'Will you wear it, Tilly? Knowing that you wear it as a sign that I belong to you and you belong to me?'

She nodded, not trusting herself to speak.

'Will you marry me? In front of our family and friends?'

She nodded again, her eyes sparkling. 'Only if you marry me back.'

His laugh filled her soul with happiness. 'I will.'

And so it was that, two months to the day after leaving the island in such a state of despair, Tilly stood before her family, her friends, and even the Wyndhams, and promised to have and to hold Rio Mastrangelo for all her life.

She didn't see them, of course. Though two hundred guests had joined them on the island, and were standing on the beach sipping champagne and adoring the obviously in love couple, Tilly saw only Rio.

She saw him as he was—the handsome billionaire who had devoted his skills to preserving buildings and objects of interest. She saw him as he had been—

the boy with too much worry on his shoulders, who had loved and felt loved by one person on earth, the person who had spent years saying a slow, painful farewell to her only child. She saw him as he would be—her life partner, her lover and, yes, the father of her children.

A smile curled her lips as she thought of the tiny life shielded in her belly.

But that was her secret. A gift she would give him later, when they were all alone.

Night fell and the guests remained. A blanket of stars shone overhead, and as Tilly pressed her body close to Rio's and he wrapped his arms around her, holding her to him, a shooting star passed directly above the party, serenading it with wishes from heaven.

Tilly blinked up at her husband and smiled.

Their future was brighter than a thousand shooting stars.

* * * * *

*In THE GAME, the second novel of
THE ICON TRILOGY, USA TODAY
bestselling romance author Vanessa Fewings
widens the canvas of the glamorous and
intoxicating world of art as Zara must make
the ultimate choice at a moment when all is
not as it seems.*

My reflection in the hotel bedroom mirror was the epitome of a young woman putting on a brave face. This Escada gown clung like spun gold to my curves and these delicate fine straps with their diamond beading caught the light; the back so low it hovered just above my butt to blend glamour with a sassy chic.

"Why did you even bring this dress?" I whispered to myself, though my eyes answered with a hope for a reconciliation with Tobias. I broke my gaze, focusing instead on my strappy high heels—the ones Tobias bought me during that wild weekend when we'd stayed at The Dorchester hotel just weeks ago.

My stomach muscles tightened with all the uncertainty.

No matter how cozy this room was with its long velvet drapes or welcoming seating area, it wasn't home. I'd spent much of the day reading everything I could about Tobias online. Not one article hinted at any misdemeanors or bad-boy behavior, unless you counted the socialites he flaunted, hanging off his arm in those glamour shots of him arriving at or leaving exclusive social events.

Of all the possible scenarios of my reunion with

him yesterday, being placed on a plane and sent back to London within moments of seeing him wasn't one of them.

Raising my chin high, I gave myself a confident nod of approval that I'd handled myself well when he'd tried to push his agenda on me. Turning my thoughts to tonight, I ran my fingers through my auburn locks that I'd styled elegantly to tumble over my shoulders, and I dabbed my soft pink lipstick as I finished applying my makeup.

I couldn't wait to be inside The Broad and it made me smile to know I was going there now. Grabbing my clutch purse and heading out of my room, I had a bounce in my step and I even rode the elevator with my newfound confidence, the residue from my phobia of lifts having eased slightly; *because of him.*

Gabe was waiting for me in the hotel foyer and his eyes widened when he saw me. "What's Rita Hayworth doing at the Sofitel?" he called out.

I responded with a confident turn and a flirty flick of my hair.

He looked gorgeous in a snazzy black tuxedo. "Almost didn't recognize you there," he said.

"Let's go see some art."

The valet brought around Gabe's blue Audi R8 and, with the inspirational music of Sia playing as an atmospheric backdrop, we drove along Beverly Boulevard.

Half an hour later we'd arrived on Grand Avenue in downtown LA and were pulling up to the striking honeycombed structure of The Broad. Gabe handed over his car keys to the valet and we headed on in.

Within minutes we were sipping bubbly from tall

flutes and sighing with happiness at being back in our natural habitat. We made our way through the well-dressed crowd who'd gathered for the reception. I paused awhile to admire the *Balloon Dog*, an enormous blue balloon-shaped masterpiece by Koons. It was such a fun piece and Gabe joked how he could only afford the miniature one sold in the gift shop.

He pointed out his young student Terrance Hill, who was greeting guests across the showroom. Gabe shared with me how the young man was fatherless and yet his inspiring talent and determination had earned him a scholarship at UCLA.

Gabe stared on proudly. "Terrance excelled in my art history class but found his true calling is modern art. He has my blessing, of course."

The bright young star with neat dreadlocks wore the brightest smile, and I guessed the pretty forty-something black woman by his side was his proud mom.

We headed on over to them to offer our congratulations.

His paintings were featured around the walls. Gabe and I took our time to admire each one and I marveled at Terrance's gift of layering colors and his use of texture. He was being hailed as a young Jackson Pollock and I could see why.

As I turned to face the crowd, my breath caught when I saw a vision of pure masculine beauty—Tobias Wilder.

He was here.

Sipping from an amber drink and looking ridiculously sharp in a black tuxedo with his hair predictably ruffled to perfection, so damn gorgeous as he

smiled his response to something a middle-aged couple were saying to him. *God*, now he was doing that
thing where he arched his brows as he listened with
sincerity, seemingly engrossed in conversation, his
left hand tucked into his trouser pocket as he leaned
forward to engage with them.

A jolt of reality hit me when I saw his ex-girlfriend
and powerhouse attorney Logan Arquette standing
beside him. She was wearing a pretty green gown
and her usual cold glare.

My body froze when Tobias's stare found me in the
crowd and his expression reflected intrigue.

Tobias and Logan strolled toward us, confidently
nodding here and there at the other guests who parted
respectfully for them.

My back straightened as they neared us and I decided to go with a customary "Mr. Wilder, nice to
see you again."

Tobias gave a warm smile. "Zara."

A seductive chill spiraled up my spine and I went
for my best stony-faced expression to match his
amused demeanor.

Wilder wore that dazzling suit as though some arti-
san had carved it over his muscular physique to high-
light his firm chest and broad shoulders, and his grin
widened just enough to hide that he was strategizing.

"It's my pleasure to introduce Professor Gabe An-
derson, art historian." I gestured to them. "Tobias
Wilder and Logan Arquette."

"Nice to see you, Zara." Logan's tone lacked sincerity and she looked triumphant as her arm wrapped
through Tobias's in a blatant gesture of possessive-

ness. Her flirting was being used against me to lessen my resolve.

"Quite the exhibition," said Tobias.

Gabe responded with praise for Tobias's own gallery and he told him how much he loved The Wilder's reputation for the exclusive exhibits they were famed for.

"We have something very special coming to The Wilder." Logan zeroed in on Gabe. "It's something you'll find particularly appealing if you love history."

"Top secret for now," added Tobias, fixing his attention on me.

The full force of his power hit me and his stare held me captive.

A memory flittered through my mind of the way he'd once touched me; a mesmerizing strength and tenderness and there came a stark recollection of the way he made me come so very hard.

Think about something else.

Anything else.

Why did he have to look at me like this? As though we weren't over.

"Please excuse me," I said. "There's a Doug Aitken piece I'm dying to see."

I felt rude for leaving Gabe with them but I needed to put distance between us. Tobias's glare was burning my back as I walked into the next room. Avoidance was probably the best way to get through tonight.

I willed myself to concentrate on the gold plaque before me. The word *now* had been enlarged to a three-dimensional wall model and was filled with a collage of images.

The last place I wanted to be was in the now.

"Zara." Tobias's voice exuded a deadly seduction.

A jolt of uncertainty trailed up my spine.

He stood a few feet away. "You look beautiful. I love that dress on you. I'm glad you wore it tonight."

I wanted to believe his words were a peace offering but the way his fierce gaze held mine reminded me of our goodbye outside The Wilder. He had that same look now in those green eyes.

I turned to go. "I have to find Gabe."

He reached out and held my wrist. "Dance with me."

He was torturing me with physical contact; his firm touch reminding me what I'd lost, his sensual grip dangerously persuasive.

"I can't."

He arched a brow. "You moved on fast."

"Gabe's a friend."

"I was worried I'd have to challenge him to a duel." He grinned devilishly. "Have you any idea how stunning you look?"

Evidently he knew how gorgeous he looked too, because he was using his magnetism to manipulate me into spending more time with him.

"Zara, dance with me."

"How did you know I'd be here?"

"I could say the same."

"The artist is one of Gabe's students."

His frown deepened. "One dance. Or…"

"Or what?"

"Don't tempt me with refusing, Leighton." He arched an amused brow. "Or there will be consequences."

"In what way?"

"I'm still a client of Huntly Pierre. Do it for them. You can always think of England." He winked.

I relented with a nod, and when his hand rested on the lower curve of my spine I resisted the desire to close my eyes and lean into him as though there was no tension between us. Tobias guided me into a cocktail lounge and led me toward the small crowd slow dancing to Nina Simone, her sultry tones setting the scene for romance.

He pulled me into a hug. "It's good to see you."

I let Tobias take the lead as I rested my right hand on his shoulder, my left sliding against his right palm, his fingers closing around mine. The way his body crushed against me felt deceptively good and caused my body to tingle deliciously. My nipples further betrayed me by hardening in response to his provocative cologne.

"I think this might be my all-time favorite gallery," I said.

"What about The Wilder?"

"What about it?"

"I suppose I deserve that."

I dragged my teeth over my bottom lip to tease him and there came a rush of exhilaration when his pupils dilated with arousal, revealing I was having the same effect on him. He waltzed me around and we fit together annoyingly well.

Why couldn't this be us? Two lovers enjoying a romantic evening without the looming inevitability of this ending badly.

"Zara, you're intoxicating." He gave a heart-stopping grin.

"Don't!" I wasn't falling for his flattery.

He spun me around and my feet became light as he whisked me along with a smooth glide. He yanked me against his firm chest and then stilled, his mouth lingering perilously close to mine. Our eyes locked on each other as the world fell away. Those specks of gold in his green irises were hypnotic.

He nuzzled close to my ear. "I'm glad you came."

I leaned back to see him better. "Tell me how to get through to you."

He tipped me backward and held me suspended in a scooped pose low in his arms as he leaned forward to whisper, "Tell me you want me."

"Everyone's watching."

"Say it." His mouth brushed mine.

I nipped his lower lip and he let out a moan of pleasure and flipped me up and yanked my body to his again, his hardness digging into my lower stomach.

He arched an amused brow. "Now we're going to have to dance until my dignity returns. I blame you."

A rush of desire at being in his arms again flooded through me. I was fast becoming drunk with arousal from the way he was holding me so masterfully.

My words spilled out in a flurry. "Mr. Wilder, you misled me—"

"No, Zara."

"If you care about me you'll not taunt me like this."

"Of course I care about you."

"What is this?"

"I'm forgiving you."

"What for?"

He looked surprised. "Your sneak attack on me tonight. I'm completely defenseless against you."

"I have to get back to Gabe."

"I will have you again," he said with an edge of danger. "I know you want that too."

The room was spinning.

Tobias's glare fixed on me fiercely as though he needed to see I wanted this. These were the words I'd craved to hear but I was past being led astray. I looked over his shoulder so I could access these remnants of strength that were evading me.

"Zara, you misjudged me. Let me prove it to you."

No, and my anguished expression told him that. "Let me go."

And let me go...

He stepped back. "Let's talk at least."

I raised my chin high, pretending he had no effect on me. He went to say something but instead he quickly broke my glare.

"I can find my own way." I rushed from him, needing to put distance between us as my heart shattered. This chill reached my bones and my mind felt dazed from the confliction of seeing him again.

Gabe waved my way to get my attention. "Looks like you've swept one of America's most wanted off his feet."

"Most wanted?"

"Bachelors," he said. "Look at him."

Tobias was standing beneath an archway and he was staring right at me, his expression marred with confusion in a haunting reminder of what could never be.

I spun around to break the intensity of Wilder's confident stance and faced one of Terrance's paintings, trying to find my center again and fight this wavering desire to believe there could be an *us*.

The plaque beside Terrance's painting stated this one was called *Unpredictable*.

The young artist had seemingly channeled his emotions onto the large canvas. It spoke in ways I couldn't define. There was freshness to it, a vibrancy and a seeming grasp of pain someone so young shouldn't know.

Perhaps seeing Tobias tonight wasn't a coincidence. *No*, surely he wouldn't hit a gallery with me here? His words of affection had been used to distract me. I'd almost fallen for him all over again.

I went in search of him, recalling Icon's MO and remembering he always cut the power before a heist.

I hurried out of the showroom with my chest tight with tension, on through the expansiveness, scanning the many faces of the guests roaming freely as I weaved my way around them.

There he was—

Sitting alone on a wooden bench and people watching, his intelligent eyes taking everything in. He glanced at his watch and then pushed himself to his feet and strolled eastward down a long hallway.

After turning a corner, I saw him standing at the end, casually leaning against a wall and scrolling through his phone. I wondered if this was how he deactivated the security system, by using some gadget app he'd invented.

With a confident stride I headed toward him. He showed surprise when he saw me.

I folded my arms. "Are you going to hit this place?"

"Don't be ridiculous."

I narrowed my eyes. "What are you up to?"

He feigned innocence. "Enjoying the art."

I stepped left to peer into the dark showroom.

His frown deepened. "You can't see that one to-night. There's a good reason it's cordoned off."

"I'm sure there is." I threw him a look of triumph and climbed over the rope and headed in, pulling the strap of my purse across my chest and easing it behind me.

Passing the first impressively large portrait on the left of a holographic tornado, I admired its realism. Though with merely digits and codes it wouldn't be worth anything and was impossible to steal. Walking onward there was the footage of a hurricane at sea with rolling waves; a living, breathing masterpiece.

My heel caught in the ground and I peered down at the tiny holes in the floor tiles.

"Hurry!" Tobias was inside the rope and frantically gesturing. "This is the rain room!"

I gawped toward the sound of rushing air.

A deluge of rain—drenching me.

When I opened my eyes, I blinked through the blur of water at a horror-stricken Tobias. The rain ceased, though a few droplets still hit my head as my hair squished to my scalp. My dress clung horribly. I'd become the exhibit.

Careful with his footing on the slippery floor, Tobias hurried over and shrugged out of his jacket.

Breathing through these waves of panic... *Oh, no*, I'd ruined this lovely dress. Wiping water out of my eyes, I looked up at him. "I'm so embarrassed."

Tobias cupped my cheeks and leaned in and kissed me, his lips soft and comforting against mine, my mouth tingling, my need for him relighted as I almost forgot this was forbidden.

He broke away and gave a reassuring tug on his jacket to bring it farther around my shoulders. "You have a funny way of trying to save me, Zara Leighton."

I gave a shrug of surrender and shivered.

Don't miss the stunning continuation of
THE ICON TRILOGY *with THE GAME,*
available in September only from HQN Books.

Get 2 Free Books,
Plus 2 Free Gifts—

just for trying the Reader Service!

HARLEQUIN *Presents*

SPECIAL EXCERPT FROM

H HARLEQUIN

Presents.

*Leonidas Betancur was presumed dead after a plane
crash, and he cannot recall the vows he made to his bride,
Susannah, four years ago. But once she tracks him down,
his memories resurface—and he's ready to collect his
belated wedding night! Susannah wants Leonidas to reclaim
his empire and free her of his legacy. But dangerously
attractive Leonidas steals her innocence with a touch…
And the consequences of their passion will bind them
together forever!*

Read on for a sneak preview of Caitlin Crews's next story
A BABY TO BIND HIS BRIDE
ONE NIGHT WITH CONSEQUENCES

There was a discreet knock on the paneled door and the
doctor stepped back into the room.

"Congratulations, madame, monsieur," the doctor said,
nodding at each of them in turn while Susannah's breath
caught in her throat. "The test is positive. You are indeed
pregnant, as you suspected."

She barely noticed when Leonidas escorted the doctor
from the room. He could have been gone for hours. When he
returned, he shut the door behind him, enclosing them in the
salon that had seemed spacious before, and that was when
Susannah walked stiffly around the settee to sit on it.

His dark, tawny gaze had changed, she noticed. It had
gone molten. He continued to hold himself still, though she
could tell the difference in that, too. It was as if an electrical
current ran through him now, charging the air all around him
even while his mouth remained in an unsmiling line.

And he looked at her as if she was naked. Stripped. Flesh and bone with nothing left to hide.

"Is it so bad, then?" he asked in a mild sort of tone she didn't believe at all.

Susannah's chest was so heavy, and she couldn't tell if it was the crushing weight of misery or something far more dangerous. She held her belly with one hand as if it was already sticking out. As if the baby might start kicking at any second.

"The Betancur family is a cage," she told him, or the parquet floor beneath the area rug that stretched out in front of the fireplace, and it cost her to speak so precisely. So matter-of-factly. "I don't want to live in a cage. There must be options."

"I am not a cage," Leonidas said with quiet certainty. "The Betancur name has drawbacks, it is true, and most of them were at that gala tonight. But it is also not a cage. On the contrary. I own enough of the world that it is for all intents and purposes yours now. Literally."

"I don't want the world." She didn't realize she'd shot to her feet until she was taking a step toward him, very much as if she thought she might take a swing at him next. As if she'd dare. "I don't need you. I don't want you. I want to be free."

He took her face in his hands, holding her fast, and this close his eyes were a storm. Ink dark with gold like lightning, and she felt the buzz of it. Everywhere.

"This is as close as you're going to get, little one," he told her, the sound of that same madness in his gaze, his voice.

And then he claimed her mouth with his.

Don't miss
A BABY TO BIND HIS BRIDE
available January 2018 wherever
Harlequin Presents® books and ebooks are sold.

www.Harlequin.com

HARLEQUIN

Presents®

Coming next month—*Prince's Son of Scandal*, the final part of Dani Collins's The Sauveterre Siblings quartet! Angelique, Henri, Ramon and Trella make up world's most renowned family—wherever they go, scandal is sure to follow. They're protected by the best security money can buy—but what happens when each of these Sauveterre siblings meets the one person who can breach their heart?

For one night, reclusive heiress Trella Sauveterre throws off the fear-ridden shackles of her childhood abduction. But after succumbing to a sizzling seduction, she becomes unexpectedly pregnant! Deeply uncomfortable in the spotlight, Trella can't bear a high-profile pregnancy and keeps the identity of her baby's father hidden…

Then a tabloid photo of a scorching kiss implicates Crown Prince Xavier of Elazar in the scandal. He'll do anything to claim his shock child—even kidnap Trella! Xavier *must* legitimize his son. And it'll be his pleasure to make Trella his royal bride!

Xavier and Trella's story
Prince's Son of Scandal
Available January 2018!

And you're sure to enjoy the first three Sauveterre siblings' stories…
Pursued by the Desert Prince
His Mistress with Two Secrets
Bound by the Millionaire's Ring
Available now!

HPBPA1217

Want to give in to temptation with
steamy tales of irresistible desire?

Check out **Harlequin® Presents®**,
Harlequin® Desire and
Harlequin® Kimani™ Romance books!

New books available every month!

CONNECT WITH US AT:

Harlequin.com/Community

 Facebook.com/HarlequinBooks

 Twitter.com/HarlequinBooks

 Instagram.com/HarlequinBooks

 Pinterest.com/HarlequinBooks

ReaderService.com

**ROMANCE WHEN
YOU NEED IT**

PGENRE2017

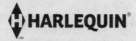